BLOODLINES

HEART OF WAR

CAPSTONE YOUNG READERS

Bloodlines is published by Capstone Young Readers,
A Capstone Imprint, 1710 Roe Crest Drive
North Mankato, MN 56003
www.capstoneyoungreaders.com

Cataloging-in-Publication Data is available on the Library of
Congress website.
ISBN: 978-1-62370-002-7 (paperback)
ISBN: 978-1-62370-042-3 (ebook)

Summary: A heart-pounding, action-packed tale of combat
and kinship skillfully crafted by United States Marine Corps
veteran and acclaimed comics writer M. Zachary Sherman
(*SOCOM: SEAL Team Seven*). Follow the Donovans through four
generations of American wars—from World War II to the War
in Afghanistan—where each explosive moment defines the
future of this military family.

Illustrated by: Fritz Casas, Raymund Bermudez, Josef Cage

Photo credits: Artistic Effects Shutterstock: lapi, Slobodan
Zivkoviv

Printed in the United States of America in
Stevens Point, Wisconsin.
052013
007383R

BLOODLINES
HEART OF WAR

M. ZACHARY SHERMAN

THE DONOVAN FAMILY

For four generations, members of the Donovan family have proudly served in the U.S. military. Follow their stories, and trace their connections, from World War II to the War in Afghanistan, where each explosive moment defines this family's future.

Courage. Strength. Tradition. Loyalty.

It's in their Bloodlines.

CONTENTS

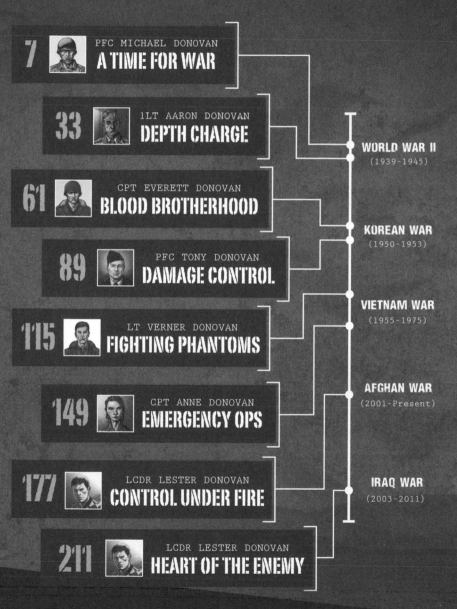

WORLD WAR II
(1939-1945)

KOREAN WAR
(1950-1953)

VIETNAM WAR
(1955-1975)

AFGHAN WAR
(2001-Present)

IRAQ WAR
(2003-2011)

PRIVATE FIRST CLASS
MICHAEL DONOVAN

ORGANIZATION:
Dog Company, 2nd Battalion, 506th
Parachute Infantry Regiment

CONFLICT: WORLD WAR II

LOCATION: CARENTAN, FRANCE

MISSION: Drop behind enemy lines,
capture the town of Carentan, France from
the German army, and secure an operations
base for Allied forces.

A TIME FOR WAR

Turbulence.

A rough ride didn't bother Private First Class Michael Donovan, but the sounds scared him half to death. Every time the C-47 Skytrain hit a pocket of air, the plane shuddered and dipped. The cabin's pop-riveted sheet-metal frame shifted and creaked. Sometimes the noises grew so loud, Private Donovan thought the entire plane would rip apart.

Flying wasn't usually a problem for the newbie soldier— neither was parachuting. He'd already done his mandatory five training drops. Donovan thought he knew what to expect. Problem was, those parachute jumps had been in clear skies over the Army Camp Toccoa in Stephens County, Georgia. Tonight, soaring 1,500 feet above the black waters of the English Channel, looked and felt a whole lot different.

Mike Donovan, sandwiched between Private Marko Peretti from Philadelphia and Sergeant Frank Anness from New York, glanced around at the other passengers. He eyed the nine soldiers of Dog Company, 2nd Battalion, 506th Parachute Infantry Regiment, 101st Airborne, 2nd Platoon. These men were just a few of more than 13,000 Allied soldiers flying toward France in carrier planes.

Their mission: drop behind enemy lines, take Hitler's troops by surprise, and disrupt German operations. Success would allow U.S. troops to land boats, men, and equipment on the beaches of Normandy. It would also create a two-front war for the Germans. With the Americans and British on one side and the Russians on the other, Hitler's troops would be right stuck in the middle.

Operation Overlord was the largest invasion in history, and the Allies' first real push into Europe. Everyone from the lowliest grunts to the silver-star generals knew the invasion would succeed. But they had to get there first, and that meant flying through some nasty turbulence.

Donovan squirmed as the C-47 Skytrain dropped thirty feet in midair and then righted itself. Nervously, he tried shifting in his seat. With more than eighty pounds of gear strapped to his body, moving wasn't easy.

The young private checked his watch. Midnight. Only fifteen more minutes until they jumped.

Next to him, Sergeant Anness leaned over and smiled. "Don't worry, kid," he said. "We'll get there soon enough." He glanced down at Donovan's wristwatch. "That's a nice piece. Who'd you steal it from?"

"I didn't steal it," Donovan replied. "My pa gave it to me." The private unfastened the watch from his wrist and flipped it over. Engraved on the back casing was a personal message from his father. It read: "Don't count every hour in the day; make every hour in the day count."

"Keep livin' that way, kid," said Sergeant Anness. "And don't you worry, we'll come home again."

"I hope so," said Donovan. He tightened his parachute straps, making sure they were ready to go.

Sergeant Anness shook his head. "Didn't you check them straps already, Donovan?" he asked.

"Yes, Sergeant," replied the private.

Anness punched Donovan on the shoulder. "Then leave them alone!" he commanded. "Them Rat-zis bit off more than they could chew, messing with us."

Donovan looked at him, concerned. "I know. But what if I can't—?" he began.

"You'll do fine, kid," Sergeant Anness interrupted. "Once we're on the ground, do your job. It's what we're trained for. You get me?"

Donovan nodded. "Got it, Sarge."

A sudden explosion rocked the right side of the aircraft, lighting the midnight sky. The plane dipped violently. All at once, the soldiers turned to the windows, eyeing the black clouds that surrounded them.

"What is that?" someone yelled from the front of the craft.

"Flak!" Lieutenant Spears shouted back.

Turbulence quickly became the least of Donovan's worries. The plane dropped once again. Outside, the sky was on fire. Flak pounded the air, and several thousand rounds of German ammunition came at them all at once. A number of the planes, having already been hit head-on, exploded in midair. Others spiraled toward a watery grave in the English Channel, their passengers desperately trying to jump to safety.

For the lucky few still in the sky, landfall was no more than a mile in front of them.

Inside the C-47 Skytrain, the copilot stuck his head out of the cockpit. "Get 'em ready, Lieutenant Spears!" he shouted.

The cabin glowed red as the jump indicator lights flicked on. The lieutenant rose and waved both hands in the air. Together, his troops stood. At the LT's orders, each soldier checked the gear on the man in front of him. The troops clasped their snap hooks onto the static line above their heads.

Dog Company was ready.

Then the red lights turned green and, one-by-one, men leaped out of the C-47. *Whoosh!* They were sucked out the door, until finally, PFC Mike Donovan, seventh in line to jump, came to the door and stepped out.

Donovan tumbled through the air. The aircraft was moving too fast. To avoid the weapons fire from the ground, the pilot had accelerated. Unfortunately for the paratroops, this was faster than any of them had ever jumped before.

Donovan shook away the blurriness. He righted himself, and his parachute fluttered open.

The private grasped the straps above his head and finally caught a glimpse of his surroundings. Filled with parachutes, the sky looked like an invasion of green jellyfish floating toward the ground.

Donovan looked up.

An anti-aircraft shell hit his carrier plane. The remains of the C-47 erupted in front of his eyes, shattering in a massive ball of flames. A moment later, red-hot wreckage whooshed past the newbie private, clipping his chute and blowing him off course.

The ground rushed up to meet him. Knees bent, Donovan hit the soil with a thud, rolled, and came up ready to fight. Problem was, his equipment bag was missing. He didn't even have a weapon.

Suddenly, Private Donovan heard noises coming from the woods behind him. He quickly curled the parachute cords and silky canopy into a ball. Then he moved for the cover of some nearby trees.

No more than fifteen yards in front of him, a German patrol of ten soldiers marched toward his last position. Even in the frost-filled night, sweat formed on Donovan's head as the Nazi troops passed by. They scanned the area with their weapons drawn.

Fear gripped the young private.

Donovan could feel his heart about to burst through his chest. Quietly, he crouched and leaned against a tree. His eyes darted for a way out.

Never had Donovan been this scared. His hands shook like the leaves above his head. Should he move? Should he stay? If there was one patrol, more would follow. And, without a weapon, he was as good as dead; Donovan knew that much.

The private waited for the German soldiers to pass. Then, as quietly as he could, he put one foot in front of the other. He crouched slowly in the dense underbrush. The air was so hushed, the breaking of one twig could alert the enemy.

Moments felt like days, but slowly Donovan gained distance on the German patrol. Finally, after more than an hour, he broke out of his crouch-walk and into a sprint. Where he was going, Donovan had no idea. For now, he'd run as far from the Germans as he could.

Tears flowed down Donovan's cheeks as he ran. He cursed himself. *Coward!* But what could he do? He didn't have a rifle, a bayonet, or even a canteen. Was he going to fight off ten of Hitler's men with his helmet?

Stopping at the edge of a clearing, Private Donovan saw a small farmhouse in the distance. The windows were boarded, and no lights shined through the cracks. The shelter looked abandoned. Glancing back to where the Nazis had been, he thought for a moment. Until he felt safe enough to move toward his platoon, this place would have to do.

Donovan moved quickly but quietly. He feared more German soldiers might be lurking in the surrounding forests. While his eyes scanned, the private could feel a strong pressure in his head from the adrenaline pumping through his veins. He was tired and scared. The instinct to stay alive was the only thing keeping him going.

Night in France wasn't like night in Willow Creek, Illinois, where Donovan grew up. It wasn't even like Georgia, where he had trained for the invasion. No, this was a pitch-black night with no stars and no moon—an alien planet, for all he knew.

Donovan continued through the dense underbrush to the deserted home. The locks on the front door were rusted out. Dust was inches thick on the porch. That suited the rookie soldier just fine.

Stepping inside, Donovan fumbled in his left cargo pocket a bit. Finally, he lit the one piece of gear that seemed had survived the jump—his flashlight. The beam of light cut the darkness as he entered and scanned the room.

Deserted was right.

No comforts here, only broken remains. A few small chairs and a small table sat in the front room. Stairs leading to the second floor were smashed and littered with holes.

Private Donovan closed the front door behind him. Then he jammed a small scrap of plywood between the interior door handle and the frame. It wasn't a permanent fix, but he hoped to stop anyone who might want to come in.

The young private sat down at the dusty table. He removed his helmet and placed it on the table next to his flashlight. The floor below him creaked as his weight stressed the old wooden planks. Looking around, he knew this place was no safe haven.

But what next? Donovan wondered.

He looked at his watch. It had only been two hours since he leaped from that plane and landed in enemy territory. Daylight wouldn't come for another few. Donovan didn't dare use the flashlight any more for fear the enemy would see it and zero in on him.

Rest and calm down, that's what I need to do, Donovan told himself. *You're alive, at least. For now...*

The young private ran a shaking hand over his sweaty crew cut, trying to figure out his next move. The platoon didn't have a backup plan in case everyone got separated. His map case was gone. But from the distant gunshots, he knew war was only a few miles away.

If he headed north, Donovan would, more than likely, meet up with other members of his platoon. But move during the daytime? Was that wise? Was it any safer than moving through occupied France at night, where the Germans had home-field advantage?

His mind raced for a solution. But soon, his eyelids drooped, and PFC Michael Donovan—paratrooper from Dog Company, 2nd Battalion, 506th Parachute Infantry Regiment, 101st Airborne, 2nd Platoon—fell asleep.

***

The sound of creaking wood awakened Donovan in heart-stopping fright. Like a shot, he was up, grabbing his helmet and looking around. Unknown by him, his flashlight had fallen off the table, hit the ground, and rolled out of his line of sight.

Through the spaces in the planks that covered the windows, he could see the shadows of men moving. The sun cut their forms into silhouettes.

Daylight! he thought. *How long have I been out?*

Quickly, Donovan looked around, studying the situation. Nowhere to run, nowhere to hide. The house was empty with not even a sheet to cover the table and hide under. His eyes glanced toward the second floor.

Creak! The sounds from outside were louder again. They were closer to the front door. Like it or not, he knew the enemy would be coming in.

Maybe they're Americans, he thought. *Lost, scared, just like me.*

The private knew he could shout the verbal signal, "Flash," to which the proper Allied response was "Thunder." However, if they were German soldiers, he'd be giving himself away.

Looking at the stairs again, Donovan knew he had to chance it. As quietly as he could, the private moved and began to climb. One foot at a time, he did his best to step as lightly as possible. The wood was badly rotted. An unsteady footfall would shatter the boards, sending him crashing to the ground and alerting his visitors.

The soldiers were at the door, rattling the handle. Almost to the top now, excitement got the better of Donovan. He slipped. His left foot fell into a hole between the second stair from the top. Desperately, the private tried to free himself. Then he heard the voices.

Donovan couldn't understand the language, but he knew what it was. *German.*

The sound of a shoulder hitting wood boomed into the small, empty house. Donovan pulled with all his might, but could not free his foot from the stairs.

He had only seconds as, over and over again, the shoulder hit. The pounding echoed all around him. Donovan pulled, twisted, and yanked, but nothing he did would free his foot.

Finally, just as the door came crashing open, the wooden stair splintered, and Donovan quickly dove around the banister. Peering down through the small holes in the wooden ceiling, the young private could see the first floor.

Nazi soldiers, three of them armed to the teeth, entered the building. They stood for a moment, guns scanning. After a long beat, they entered farther. One room at a time, they split up and secured the first floor.

Deciding the house was empty, two of the Nazis removed their helmets. They entered the small living room where the table and chairs sat.

Just then, one of the Nazi soldiers stopped and nodded at the stairs.

His fellow soldier smiled back, pointed to the rotting wood, and shrugged. The stairs were in such bad shape, he obviously figured there was no way anyone could be up there.

Grinning, he peered upward.

With a pull of the trigger, the soldier blasted ammo randomly through the ceiling.

Tightening the grip on his legs, Donovan curled himself into a small ball. The bullets ripped up through the floor all around him. He wanted to scream—to yell out—but he didn't.

The German laughed and continued spraying bullets into the ceiling. After a moment, he shouldered the weapon, took out a pack of cigarettes, and offered one to each of the others. All three of them lit up.

Hopefully, Donovan thought, *they won't look up at their smoke trails.* The Nazis would see him clear as day through the holes in the ceiling.

Time passed as the Germans enjoyed their moments away from the war. They were calm and relaxed, taking an unauthorized break from patrolling the woods.

Not Donovan. He was a bundle of nerves. At any second, the Germans might look up, notice his shape, and he'd be dead.

His legs began cramping from being balled up. He didn't dare shift. Even the slightest movement could cause the ceiling to creak, drawing the enemy's gaze upward. If he didn't move, didn't make a sound, and as long as they didn't come upstairs, he'd be safe. Or so he thought. And that's when he saw it.

His flashlight. The army-issued flashlight was still under the table. It was only a matter of time before the Germans spotted it and began searching for him.

Donovan's pulse quickened. His hands began to shake again. The young private's eyes darted from side to side, looking for a way out. But there was nothing he could do. If he as much as breathed heavily, he'd be discovered.

Private Donovan watched as the shooter bent down to tighten his bootlace and froze. Squinting, the Nazi didn't recognize it at first. As he slowly reached out and picked up the flashlight, he knew exactly what it was. Eyes wide, the German soldier sat up and looked at his friends.

"*Amerikaner!*" he shouted. "*Amerikaner!*"

The Germans' guns came up, and they went on alert. Donovan's world exploded in a hail of bullets that pierced the farmhouse and shattered the wood.

But these shots weren't aimed at him. These shots came from outside.

Huddled in a ball, Donovan screamed as lead splintered the flooring around him. All at once, the German soldiers were racked with rounds, fell to the ground, and stopped breathing.

"Flash!" someone yelled from outside.

Donovan looked down from his perch. He was shocked to be alive and to hear an American voice.

"Thunder! Thunder!" the young private yelled back.

Creeping down the stairs, Donovan looked as PFC Peretti and Sergeant Anness of Dog Company popped their heads around the frame of the front door.

"Sarge!" Donovan yelled.

Eyes wide, Anness came in the doorway. "Donovan?"

The men shook hands.

"What the heck happened to you?" asked Anness.

"Yeah, how'd you end up here?" Peretti added. He watched Donovan reach down and retrieve his flashlight from the floor.

"When the plane exploded," Donovan began, "I was blown off course. I missed the drop zone." He didn't dare tell them of his incredible fear.

"Really? I thought we were supposed to drop into this farmhouse full of Germans," Private Peretti joked. He laughed as Anness jabbed him in the side, sensing Donovan's anxiety.

"Don't worry, kid. It's okay," said Sergeant Anness.

Donovan continued, "I lost my musette bag, my map, my rifle, everything. After I hit the ground last night, I saw this place, and thought I'd wait until someone found me."

"Yeah, half our entire invasion force is scattered across France," Sergeant Anness explained. "Lieutenant Spears ordered us to recon the area to look for 'em. Glad we found you!" The sergeant reached down and took one of the German's MP40 machine guns. He handed it to Donovan. "You'll need this," he said.

Donovan looked up. "We lose anyone?"

Peretti's eyes quickly saddened. "Yeah," he said after a moment. "Lots."

Donovan nodded and flipped off the safety on the MP40. "Where are we going now?" he asked.

"Listen…" Sergeant Anness replied with a smile. He pointed toward the sound of cannon fire in the distance. "That-a-way," he said.

***

The rally point wasn't as far as Private Donovan thought. If he had mustered the courage to move last night, Donovan could have regrouped with his platoon in under an hour.

Sergeant Anness and Private Peretti had gone this way before. They had rescued other lost paratroops and had the route memorized. Thousands of men had been blown off course and, to the luck of the Allies, this complete failure had turned into a major advantage.

"Caught the Nazis totally off guard with the drops," Peretti explained to Donovan. "The best part? We completely disrupted all of the German outposts. With a million of us running around like crazy, the Germans don't know where to shoot. Confusion helped us get some heavy equipment up onto the beaches, but our reinforcements are—"

Movement in the nearby trees made him go quiet.

Holding up a closed fist, Private Peretti silently ordered the men to stop. Opening a hand, he waved his palm toward the ground. He signaled all three soldiers to go into a crouch.

Private Donovan looked at his own hand. It began shaking again. He made a tight fist, trying to stop it. He couldn't.

The rustling was getting closer.

"Flash!" shouted Peretti. No response came back.

"FLASH!" he shouted again.

Nearby, Sergeant Anness raised his Thompson machine gun to his shoulder, ready to fire.

Just then, a muffled "Thunder!" came out of the forest in front of them.

Standing, the trio was pleasantly surprised to see Private "Popeye" Wynne and Private Gordon emerge from the trees. Both men were from Easy Company.

Sergeant Anness smiled. "Look what we found," he said, pointing at Donovan.

"Nice to see ya, kid," said Popeye. "We're over here."

***

The road to the town of Angoville-Au-Plain changed quickly from a deserted tree-lined path to a village buzzing with American activity. Soldiers and troopers from every company, Easy to Dog, and most of the entire 2nd Battalion had assembled here in the town square.

As they walked in, Donovan noticed groups of soldiers on the grassy berms. They laughed, ate chow, and milled around like they were on vacation.

All of this felt wrong. In fact, nothing had gone right since wheels-up in England. Donovan wasn't sure if it ever really would. Everything was a failure. The plan, the insertion, the drop. *Heck,* he thought, looking down at his shaking hand. *I'm carrying a German machine gun, for Pete's sake.* Had none of them been through what he had? Had none of them been as scared as he had been?

Donovan asked himself these questions as he regrouped with the other members of his platoon at the company assembly area and checked in with his sergeant. They were excited to see him alive. Even though they invited him to relax with them as they ate, Donovan felt strangely detached from his friends. He slowly shuffled away from the others, alone. He felt like they were all looking at him, like they knew he had hidden in that farmhouse to get away from the war.

Donovan fought back the tears as his mind drifted away from France, away from the war, and back to home. Walking off by himself, he reached into his left jacket pocket and pulled out a piece of paper. He unfolded the dirty, worn envelope. It was a well-read letter from his fiancee, Renee.

Slumping onto the ground, the tears came freely now. Donovan wondered if he was ever going to get home to see her. He clasped a hand over his mouth, trying to keep quiet, when he heard someone approach.

"Can I sit?" said a voice from behind.

Donovan saw Sergeant Anness come out of the shadows. The sergeant had a duffle bag slung over his shoulder. Donovan nodded a silent "yes" as the sergeant sat next to him.

"I know what you did, Private," Anness said, reaching into the bag. "And I know it's eating at you."

Donovan looked at him. "What do you—?"

"Hiding in the farmhouse," Anness continued. "I jumped out right after you and saw where you landed. By the time I got to your position, you were gone. Soon after, I got picked up by members of Easy Company."

"I was so scared!" Donovan explained. "I was more scared than I ever was in my whole life, Sarge."

"I know, kid, and I'm not here to make you feel guilty," said Anness. "Heck, I might have done the same."

"I'm a coward," Donovan said through the tears.

Looking down at Donovan's hands, Anness saw the letter he held tightly. "You're not a coward," he replied. "You were trapped with three German soldiers and no weapon. You were scared, and I understand. We all do. But we're here now, on the front lines, and no amount of wishing or praying's going to change that.

"You need to reach deep down inside you," the sergeant continued. "Find that courage to carry on and hold on to it tight. That's the only way you're going to get back home—to make it through this alive."

Donovan nodded as the sergeant stood.

"We're not here for the pay or the chow," added Anness. "We're here for each other. We do what do so the guy on the left and the guy on the right can go home again. Understood?"

"Yes, Sarge," Donovan replied.

"Good," said Anness. He offered a hand and helped Donovan up from the ground. "Then I need you."

After unslinging a gun from his shoulder, Anness handed it over to Donovan. Then he gave him a bandoleer full of ammo.

"Easy Company's been tasked to take out four German 88 anti-aircraft guns that're pounding the beaches," said the sergeant. "Lieutenant Spears wants us to assist with an ammo drop. You'll be with me on the heavy as my backup along the tree line. Weapons and ammo only. Leave everything else."

Donovan nodded. He slapped a magazine into the receiver, racked the action, and readied the gun to fire with a loud clack.

The sound jolted Donovan's nerves a bit. "Okay."

Nearby, Anness loaded his M1 Garand rifle. "Then let's move out," commanded the sergeant.

***

Donovan moved through the forest with the eight other members of Dog Company. Standing in the center of a tactical column formation, he tried desperately to keep his fear in check. He concentrated on anything other than the sounds of thunder coming from in front of them.

But it didn't help. Every snapping branch or rustling leaf made his heart jump and head swivel.

The explosions and firing got louder as the men approached a clearing. The opening was forty yards square, surrounded by tall trees. At the far end, three of the four howitzer cannons were placed so they could angle in on the beach for German fire support. The fourth and final cannon was set back at a ninety-degree angle from the first.

Through the trees, Donovan watched the third 88 explode as members of Easy Company ran through the trenches that connected the massive cannons. Germans flooded the area with bullets from the tree lines and the far end of the trenches. They were trying anything to halt the American attack.

Lieutenant Spears stopped and raised a hand. Like a third base coach, he silently signaled his men what to do.

On his command, they split up. He and five others went toward the third cannon where Easy Company was pinned down. Donovan and Anness moved left, behind the cover of a small berm.

Once in position, Sergeant Anness pulled up a heavy machine gun and placed its tripod on the grass. Handing him a belt of ammo, Donovan got ready to load the Browning M1919 medium machine gun.

Then suddenly, hot lead whizzed by their ears. Bullets chipped and splintered the trees. They embedded themselves in the thick, French dirt right in front of the Americans. Twenty German soldiers, only forty yards away, began firing everything from MG42s to MP40s over the area.

Anness yelled to Donovan, "Get that belt in there!"

Donovan jammed the ammo belt into the machine gun. The gun's holding bar at the entrance of the feedway grabbed and held it in place. Ratcheting the handle, Donovan nervously looked over at Anness.

"Go!" shouted the sergeant.

The machine gun sprang to life. It threw bullets at the enemy and spit empty brass shells to the ground. Across the knoll, Germans twisted and fell as the slugs struck their bodies.

At the same time, a German stick grenade soared through the air. It landed behind Anness and Donovan with a thud. They both stared at each other.

"Grenade!" shouted Sergeant Anness.

The grenade exploded, creating a massive crater in the ground and showering the pair with rocks and soil. Anness kept firing, but Donovan, shaken by the concussion, rolled and slipped into the hole. He covered his head and pulled on his helmet to protect his face.

"What's wrong?!" Anness yelled. "Are you hit?"

Donovan cowered in the hole, frozen with fear and crying.

"Are you hurt?!" Sergeant Anness asked again.

Donovan shook his head. "No! I'm just—"

"Then get up!" Anness shouted. "Come on! Get up!"

Slowly, Donovan looked up at Anness, who was standing, firing his machine gun and facing the enemy. He was powerful, optimistic, full of confidence. Eyeing his sergeant, Donovan wondered if he'd ever be that way.

The firing was so intense that Donovan didn't know what to do. He wanted to move, but his legs wouldn't let him.

"Fire your weapon!" yelled Anness. "Pour it on 'em!"

Finally, Donovan rose, his weapon clutched in his hands. Like a crutch, he leaned on it for support.

From a distance, he could see Lieutenant Spears slide in next to Lieutenant Winters, the chief officer of Easy Company. Handing off bags of ammo, Spears got a nod from Lieutenant Winters. Then, under the cover of fire support, Spears ran off. He was followed by the five other Dog Company soldiers sprinting down the trench line.

But suddenly, Spears did something unexpected. He got out of the cover of the trench, running along the top of it, followed by the five other soldiers. Three of them were killed instantly when the German's took their shots.

Five more German soldiers stood up from the cover of the tall grass in the field. They prepared to finish off Spears and the rest of the men.

Anness screamed, "Covering fire!"

Donovan could see the Germans bearing down on the U.S. troops. They had only seconds. That's when it happened. All around Donovan, the battle slowed. The butt of his rifle pushed tightly to his shoulder, Donovan took aim and put pressure on the trigger.

Brass casings flipped out of his weapon as it discharged.

Fifty yards away, a Nazi's shoulder jerked. He twisted backward and fell to the ground.

Another squeeze and second German dropped.

Anness grinned. "That's it, Donovan! Keep it—"

But his calls of inspiration were cut short as bullets racked Anness's body.

Donovan looked over to see his sergeant, his friend, collapse to the ground. Dead.

Ahead of him, the three remaining Germans had zeroed in on their position and were firing.

Instantly, Donovan was on the machine gun, pulling the trigger. His fury boiled over. With the power of the weapon fueling his emotions, he let out a yell from the bottom of his gut. A war cry like no other came from his lungs as he mowed down the three remaining German soldiers.

Dropping the machine gun, Donovan went to Sergeant Anness's side. "Sarge?! Sarge!" he shouted.

Donovan put pressure on the wounds, but it was too late.

Anness was gone.

Donovan began to cry again. He'd never lost a friend before, and he didn't know what to do. Looking down, his hands were covered in the sticky life-giving liquid that flowed from his friend's body. He noticed they were shaking, but this time it wasn't fear that made them tremble. It was anger.

Another explosion drew his attention. The Americans blew the barrel of the last howitzer to shreds. Smoke poured out of it like a chimney. Then the shooting began to slow.

Private Donovan could hear Lieutenant Winters yelling, "Cease fire! Pull back! Everyone back to battalion!"

And like that, the battle was over.

A crunch of leaves behind him made Donovan spin, his weapon held high.

"Whoa!" said Lieutenant Spears as he and Peretti raised their hands in the air.

Peretti's face sunk as he looked down and saw Anness's body. "Sarge," said the soldier.

"We'd better get him back," interrupted Spears. The Lieutenant and Peretti reached for the body, but Donovan stood, blocking their path.

"No," Donovan said. "I'll do it, sir."

Lieutenant Spears narrowed his eyes and shouldered his weapon. "You sure, kid?" he asked.

"I'll take care of him, sir," replied Donovan. "I owe him that much."

Bending over, the young private wiped away the dirt from Anness's lifeless face. Then he lifted him off the ground.

"Come on, Sarge," he whispered. "You're going home."

***

As they returned, night fell on the staging area in Angoville-Au-Plain. Word that the 2nd Battalion had secured Sainte-Marie-du-Mont spread like wildfire throughout the ranks. Elements of the 4th Division were beginning to move men and equipment inland from the beaches. Meanwhile, M4 Sherman tanks rolled through town, and men loaded up the five-ton trucks that had made it off Omaha's sandy grave.

Even though the majority of the 101st were still scattered across Normandy, they were ordered to pack their belongings. Dog Company was preparing to move out again.

One of the privates walked the lines, asking the men if any of them had mail they wanted to send out before they got back into the fight. Several did and slipped the soldier letters, small packages, or even postcards made from pieces of cardboard— anything to get word home that they were still alive.

Donovan rolled Anness's blanket into a ball. He stuffed it and the rest of the sergeant's personal belongings into a cardboard box.

Peretti looked over at him. "Sarge's stuff?" he asked.

Donovan nodded. "Yeah," the private replied. "I thought his Jenny would want it."

"Thoughtful of you," said Peretti.

Donovan tied the package with a string. As he turned over his wrist to knot it, the young private caught a glimpse of the watch his father had given him.

"Crap!" he said as he eyed its face. The watch itself was still ticking, keeping perfect time, but the glass was cracked.

He removed it and read the inscription again: "Don't count every hour in the day; make every hour in the day count."

A slight grin curled his lips. Donovan finally understood its meaning as he placed the watch in a small box of his own and sealed it with a freshly written letter.

Peretti nodded at the package, looking confused.

"What're you doing with your watch?" he said.

"In case I don't make it," Donovan replied. "I want Renee to have it."

"Why?" Peretti asked.

"I want her to remember me not as the man everyone thought me to be," said Donovan, "but the man I actually became."

Peretti smiled. "A little worse for wear, but still alive?"

"Something like that, yeah," said the private.

"All right, people, let's move out!" shouted Lieutenant Spears, jumping into the front seat of a Willys Jeep. "Coup de Ville isn't going to free itself!"

Scrambling, men began leaping into trucks as Donovan and Peretti piled into the back of a M3 Half-track. Looking out at the organized chaos, Donovan spotted the private gathering the mail and called him over. Handing him the packages, he thanked the young man. Then he settled back into his seat.

The young private looked up at him. "Where y'all off to now?" he asked.

Donovan looked up at the night's sky, flashes of fire illuminating the darkness.

"Listen." Donovan smiled and pointed toward the sound of cannon fire in the distance. "That-a-way," he said.

FIRST LIEUTENANT
AARON DONOVAN

ORGANIZATION:
U.S. Army, Office of
Strategic Services

CONFLICT: WORLD WAR II

LOCATION: GILLELEJE, DENMARK

MISSION: Sneak aboard the German U-505 submarine anchored off the coast of Denmark, steal the Nazi's secret codebooks, and escape alive.

DEPTH CHARGE

"Are you sure about this, Lieutenant?" General Magruder asked. He clutched a secret radio transcript in his hands.

"Yes, sir," answered First Lieutenant Aaron Donovan. "It's been rechecked and verified, sir." He squinted as he stood in front of his commanding officer. Bright orange sunlight streamed through the drapes behind the general. The sun was setting in Istanbul. The squint couldn't be helped, but it gave the young lieutenant an expression of steely determination. It was an expression that the general noted with approval.

As director of the Office of Strategic Services in Istanbul, Turkey, General Richard Magruder oversaw a delicate mission. He commanded U.S. troops that served as spies only a stone's throw from the enemy's backyard, Nazi Germany.

"Tell me the story," ordered the general. He moved from the window and sat behind his huge oak desk.

Donovan handed him a folder containing several photos of a German submarine. "She's sub U-505, sir," he said. "British destroyers stalked her for fifteen hours in the North Sea before she disappeared. It looks like her main engine gave out." Donovan pointed at the top photo. "From the dark cloud around her aft section, we assume she's leaking fuel and is disabled. This presents us with an amazing opportunity, sir."

"An intelligence opportunity?" asked the general.

"Exactly, sir," answered Donovan. "As you know, the Germans have added more decoding wheels to their Enigma cipher machine, destroying our ability to decode their messages. But the latest codebooks for every variation of the machine are onboard that sub. If we can get our hands on those codebooks, we'd be able to listen in on the Germans from here to Christmas."

The general grinned. "Where is the sub now?"

"Docked in Gilleleje," replied Donovan. "It's a small fishing village on the east coast of Denmark. WAVE picked up a radio broadcast from the U-boat skipper asking for a special engineering team be sent from Germany to help with repairs."

"I assume you have a plan," the general said.

"We're calling it Operation Deep Six," Donovan answered confidently. "With British help, we'll insert a two-man commando team to intercept those engineers and replace them. Most of the sub's forty-five-man crew will be ashore, with minimal security left on board. While pretending to repair the ship, our men will plant explosives on her ballast tanks, simulate an engine rupture, and scuttle the boat.

Then, when the rest of the crew evacuate, our men grab the codebooks and escape."

"And the Brits? Why are we cutting them in on this?"

"They've got contacts in the Danish Resistance that we'll need to successfully get out of Denmark. They've also got an experienced agent who knows these U-boats inside and out. A British commando named Nigel Brett. But it'll still go according to our plan, sir," Donovan said.

"Good work, Lieutenant." The general looked up at the young man and smiled. "When do you leave?"

Donovan's eyes went wide.

**

"Why me?" Donovan mumbled, sitting inside a C-47 Skytrain military transport.

"Because you opened your mouth, sir," said Sergeant Hawkesworth of the British Royal Air Force. "That's how the military works—Yank, Brit, or otherwise!"

"What do you mean?" Donovan asked.

"When it's your plan, you end up doing the volunteering without even knowin' it, sir!" said Hawkesworth.

Donovan grinned at the jumpmaster and shifted his seat on the bench. Hawkesworth walked away as another Brit squeezed past him. The new man stood six feet tall, one hundred eighty pounds, and was packed with the same combat gear loading down Donovan. But on him, the American decided, it looked natural.

The Brit was Captain Nigel Brett, British Commando and MI6 agent. His blond hair was cut close to the scalp. He carried his helmet at his side. At first glance, any Allied soldier would have mistaken Brett for a Nazi.

Luckily, that was the plan.

Having been in the war for the past three years, since the British troops began fighting in earnest, Brett had seen a lot of combat. Name a strategic battle and Brett had been neck-deep in it. And always fighting behind enemy lines.

Donovan's entry to the war had been completely different. After the attack on Pearl Harbor, the three Donovan brothers went to the nearest Army recruiting station to sign up. But when recruiters found out Aaron could speak fluent German, they figured the incredible education in the young man's head would be better suited for the new Intelligence Section, rather than getting spilled out on some French farm somewhere.

Michael ended up in the 101st. Everett, who always wanted a bigger challenge, hitched up with the Marine Corps. But for Aaron, the U.S. Army was a perfect fit.

Intelligence work in the Office of Strategic Services, he soon discovered, demanded more of him than just book smarts. Training involved advanced small arms, explosives, knife fighting, boxing—the works. He was learning to be a spy. Then Lieutenant Donovan was made a Lead Analyst, shipped to the Counter Intelligence center in Istanbul, Turkey, and much to his displeasure, placed behind a desk.

For two years he did his part, from advanced code breaking to signals intelligence. Donovan wanted to see more action, but he accepted each task and did the best job he could. And because of this, his peers respected him and his superiors trusted him. Now, however, the desk was gone. The war had grown closer.

The vibrations from the C-47 Skytrain's props shuddered through Donovan's entire body. *Be careful what you ask for,* he told himself.

Captain Brett sat down next to Donovan and smiled. "Glad to see all you Yanks aren't as gung-ho as General Patton back in '42!" Brett said.

"No, but we do our duty all the same," Donovan replied.

"Good," said Brett.

Anxiously, Donovan felt his parachute straps, making sure they were locked in place. Once a jumper secures his gear, he knew, he never went over it again. That was for nervous, untrained soldiers. Rechecking was a total rookie mistake.

Brett was watching him. "How many jumps will this be for you, Lieutenant?" the British captain asked.

"Seventeen," Donovan said.

Brett leaned in closer. "How many combat jumps?"

Donovan answered quietly, "None."

"For the love of—! Listen carefully," said Brett. "I was doing this long before Uncle Sam decided to join the party, so if you get me killed, I'm going to haunt you. You understand me?"

On the battlefield eight hundred feet below, First Lieutenant Donovan would have operational control over this mission. Superior officer or not, Brett reported to him—not the other way around.

"I may not have the same experience—" Donovan started.

"You've got that right," Brett interrupted.

"Which is exactly the point," continued Donovan. "I want men around me who have more experience. Who wouldn't? I specifically requested you for this operation because of your expertise. But I have trained for this, and I was put in charge. So if you're not ready to follow this operation to the letter, you can sit in this tin can while I go down there and secure the codebooks myself. Do you understand me, Captain?"

"Aye...sir." Brett raised an eyebrow and grinned. "You do at least speak German?"

"Of course," answered Donovan.

"Fine. It's your plan, and you're in command. But remember—" Brett motioned to the barrel of the Sten Mk2(S) machine pistol strapped to Donovan's gear. "This end gets pointed at the Nazis."

"Thanks," said Donovan. "I'll try to remember that."

"Thirty seconds!" the jumpmaster yelled from the cockpit. The two officers glared at one another.

"After you, sir." Brett waved toward the hatch.

Sneering, Donovan stood, clipped his snap hook onto the static line, and moved toward the open door.

The midnight wind whipped through his hair as Donovan stepped into the doorway. He jammed on his helmet and waited for the go signal.

The light turned from red to green.

"Jump!"

He swallowed hard, stepped into the roaring darkness, and let gravity take control.

***

The night was crisp. Rain clouds loomed overhead. A cool breeze blew in from the ocean to the northwest.

But Donovan didn't feel it. Sweat poured down his forehead as the two Allied commandos silently slinked north toward the small village of Gilleleje. The sweat dripped down the black greasepaint he and Brett had applied to their faces as soon as they landed. Black knit caps curled atop their crew cuts. Dark as shadows, the men each carried a black rucksack, a compact leather utility belt, and a submachine gun.

They blended perfectly into the moonless night.

Making as little noise as possible, Donovan followed the footsteps of his partner as Brett cautiously took point. At every sixth step across the damp ground, Donovan looked behind them. He stared at the dense foliage and rustling pine trees.

Denmark, he thought as he glanced around. *Not all that different from Willow Creek, Illinois.*

Except that Illinois wasn't occupied by the German army, or policed by the ruthless Gestapo. Donovan and Brett didn't need to worry about roving patrols of infantry and tanks like the men fighting on the front lines of other European battlefields, but there were many Danes who sympathized with the Germans. If the two were seen by anyone, even Danish locals, they ran the risk of being caught. The mission would be a failure.

Brett, Donovan decided, was a pompous jerk, but he was right about one thing. Donovan was green. He wasn't a field operative with years of battle-hardened missions under his belt, and tonight he was nervous. Nervous about the unknown. About the possibility of getting killed. But more importantly, Donovan was worried about not getting the job done.

Donovan felt the weapon in his palms, wondering if he'd actually have to fire it. He shook his head and wiped sweat from his eyes. Then he cleared his mind of doubt and focused again on the immediate task.

The lieutenant took deep breaths and watched Brett's boots as he followed closely through the pitch-black forest toward the port of Gilleleje.

After three hours, a break in the tree line caught Brett's attention. He signaled Donovan to crouch low. They had reached the road to the village.

Donovan knelt and raised his weapon to his shoulder.

Brett placed his back against a tree and pulled a small map from his right cargo pocket. Unfolding it, he glanced around. This part of the road wasn't paved, but it was well marked.

Brett was looking for a waypoint, a landmark. He saw a small white road marker. He looked at the luminous dial of his watch. This was the location of their ambush, but they were behind schedule. They needed to set up quickly.

Brett waved his hand in the air like a crazed third-base coach. Donovan read the signals. Brett wanted the young lieutenant to cross the road, make his way to the far side, set up cover just inside the line of trees, and wait.

Donovan sprinted across the road and hunkered down. The sound of an engine rumbled through the silent woods. Moments later, headlights illuminated the darkened dirt road. A German Volkswagen Kübelwagen drove around a bend. As the car headed straight for them, its tailpipe belched thick clouds of black smoke. It approached the ambush point.

The two Allies had gotten there just in time.

Brett locked eyes with Donovan. Brett stared at him sternly and then slid back the bolt of his gun. Across the road, Donovan did the same. Then he saw Brett reach into a pouch on his utility belt.

With the flick of a wrist, several spikes soared from Brett's hand and littered the road. The sound of the metal was muffled in the hard dirt and could not be heard above the engine of the German car.

The Kübelwagen's front left tire suddenly exploded in a small puff of white dust. The vehicle lost control. It skidded onto the muddy shoulder, a mere yard from Donovan.

The doors opened with a burst of angry German. The driver and his passenger bent over the wheel wells to inspect the damage. The driver suddenly stopped. His boot scraped against something in the dirt. He reached down and picked up a road spike. His eyes went wide.

"*Gewehre!*" he yelled.

The Germans reached for the black Lugers at their belts. Then Donovan and Brett sprang from cover and fired.

Silenced shots spit from the weapons. Donovan saw the impact and heat from each slug. The Germans' knees buckled, and then both men dropped to the ground.

Then, as suddenly as it had started, the battle was over. Silence reclaimed the forest. Donovan looked across the narrow road at Brett. Though he tried to hold back, Donovan's emotions were too powerful to stay bottled up. His bottom lip quivered. His hands shook as he gripped the submachine gun. Then tears streaked from his eyes.

"First time?" Brett asked him quietly.

Donovan nodded slowly. He reached up and wiped the wetness from his cheeks.

"It gets easier," Brett said. He slung his weapon and gripped the armpits of the nearest dead German. Then he dragged the limp figure off the road and into the shadows of the nearby trees.

Donovan looked down at the body of the second Nazi lying on the ground. "That's what scares me," he said softly.

***

Winds off the Baltic Sea weren't especially cold that time of year, but First Lieutenant Donovan sat shivering in the front seat of the Kübelwagen. Having wiped the black greasepaint from their faces, he and Brett were now wearing exact copies of the German engineers' uniforms. Donovan shuffled slowly through the personal effects they'd pulled off the bodies: I.D. papers, travel documents, handwritten letters to loved ones that would never be sent.

Brett could tell it was eating at the young American. "Shake it off, Yank. Had to be done," said the captain. He steered the stolen vehicle through the countryside.

It's not that easy, thought Donovan. He'd killed a man in cold blood. No matter the reasons, that German was dead and it was his fault. "They were just standing there, defenseless. How could we—" the first lieutenant began.

Brett slammed on the brake. "We're soldiers," he shouted. "We've taken an oath to stop Hitler from taking over this planet. If killing a couple of Nazi engineers gets us one step closer to that goal, then I'll do it again with a smile on my face. Now either get on board or get out!"

Brett's blue eyes gleamed like steel in the early morning light. A long moment passed. Brett took a deep breath and let it out slowly. "We're at war," he said softly. "We do things we're not always proud of." Donovan wasn't looking at him, but the Brit's voice seemed to change. "Lots of things."

Brett stepped on the gas.

"Yeah?" said Donovan quietly.

"Let's just say I'm not getting into heaven any time soon. But my son will. A long time from now, and not at the hands of some dirty SS Stormtrooper." Brett turned onto a paved road. "You asked, 'how could we?'"

Donovan nodded.

"I'll tell you how. I do it for my son. I do it for Ian," said the captain.

Donovan stared out the windshield. Brett's remarks reminded him of what his teacher back at the academy had said: "The needs of the many outweigh the needs of the few."

He and Brett were specks of dust in this war. Each soldier was called on to give everything, and it was all to protect a greater good. The families back home. The townspeople of Gilleleje. The freedom of whole countries, like Denmark. His and Brett's lives earned meaning by their deeds and sacrifices.

"I—" Donovan started, but there were no words, and the lieutenant played it off. "I, uh, can't see. It's too dark in here." Donovan held up the documents, trying to read them better.

Brett reached into his pocket, produced a brass lighter, and handed it to Donovan.

"Impressive," Donovan said as he struck a flame.

"My father gave me that," said Brett. "He kept it until he came back from Germany in 1919. I'll pass it on to my son, but hopefully he never has to use it like we are."

Donovan returned his attention to the pile in his lap. "Personal papers, passes, engineering specs for the sub," he mumbled, flipping through it. "Orders."

He cracked open the envelope and read the commands carefully. Suddenly, he smiled. "Yes, we got the right men," Donovan said.

"Hooray for our side," said Brett, dryly.

Donovan fished out a set of papers from his gear. He compared them to the ones found on the Germans.

Perfect, he thought. The studio shots of Brett and Donovan were an exact match in texture, grain, and lighting to the Nazi photographs. He was proud of his men. They had worked long and hard on these forgeries.

"What's our exit strategy?" Brett asked.

"Once we exit the sub, Danish Resistance will meet us on shore in a truck with a Blue Star Vodka logo," said Donovan. "They'll take us cross-country to an airstrip. A small plane will fly us to England."

"Excellent," replied Brett. "Look, we've got about two hours before we hit the village. Try to get some rest."

After folding the papers, Donovan placed them in his shirt and crossed his arms. Within seconds, he was asleep.

***

The rising sun crested over the waters of Gilleleje, casting a golden glow on the small fishing village. The town's citizens were already awake and moving. Men of all ages prepared fishing nets and carried poles to boats as the trawlers readied to cast off.

All in all, it was a very picturesque morning. Except for the steel behemoth docked not too far away. The gunmetal gray submarine U-505 sat like a wounded whale in the harbor, its hull baking in the hot sun. On the sub's deck, a twin 20-mm Flack anti-aircraft gun was manned by a single German soldier, watching over the boat for any signs of trouble from air or land. The deck officer was perched atop the conning tower, scanning the shoreline through a pair of field glasses.

On the road next to the dock sat the Kübelwagen. Donovan and Brett geared up as they looked across the water at the sub. Since the U-505 was 100 yards away from the dock, anchored in deeper waters, they would have to pilot a small rowboat over to the ship and embark from there.

"Just as I thought," Donovan said in German. "We'll have to row out to her. The port's too shallow."

"You ready?" Brett asked in German as he slid the bricks of dynamite into Donovan's satchel.

First Lieutenant Donovan adjusted his engineering uniform. "Let's go," he confirmed.

The two men emerged from their vehicle and walked toward the dock. Brett scanned every detail, mentally creating an escape route in case something went wrong. An empty rowboat lay several yards away.

A German soldier stepped in front of them. "Papers, please, gentlemen," he said in German.

Donovan and Brett reached into their pockets. They presented the soldier with their forged documents.

Slowly, casually, Brett reached into the pockets of his jacket as if he were warming his hands. In the right pocket nestled a small Walther PPK, fully loaded. The sleek pistol was German-made, but it could do just as much damage in an American hand.

The soldier carefully read through the documents. He looked the men over slowly. Brett and Donovan returned his gaze, expressionless. Finally, the German smiled, and handed back their papers.

"The captain will be happy to see you." He motioned to the small boat. "Climb aboard."

Two hours later, Donovan and Brett were neck-deep in grease, oil, and charred engine parts in the cramped rear of the sub. They were doing what they could to "affect repairs." At least, that's what they hoped all their banging and ripping apart and German cursing looked like to an outsider.

Donovan had a simple knowledge of engines. He had fixed cars in high school. Luckily, Brett knew considerably more. He had attended engineer training with MI6 agents and knew how to sabotage German equipment as well as repair it.

The U-505's chief engineer peered over his shoulder and scratched his head. "So?" he asked.

Brett shook his head. "Not good. She'll need dry-dock to make her seaworthy," he began.

"You'll be lucky to get to France without some English ship sinking you," Donovan finished, faking his disappointment with the machine.

"Batteries could get us to Norway, but not to France, yes?" asked the German.

Donovan nodded.

The German engineer rolled his eyes. "See? That is what I told the captain. But no, he wanted specialists from Berlin to tell him."

"Absolutely," Donovan said. "We hear that all the time."

"We're all just doing Hitler's bidding, eh?" said Captain Brett, jokingly.

The engineer squinted. It seemed an odd phrase, one a high-ranking German engineer wouldn't say. "Yes. Where did you say you were from?" the engineer asked suspiciously.

First Lieutenant Donovan looked at his wristwatch. "We've got work to do, and we're running out of time," he snapped. "Now either help us, or get out of the way."

Startled at Donovan's tone, the chief engineer stumbled slightly as he took a step back and saluted. "Yes, sir. I'm sorry, I didn't mean to insult you."

And with that, he was gone.

Grinning, Brett turned from the engine. "Nice one," he whispered.

"Thanks. Here." Donovan handed him the satchel with the dynamite. "Set timers for 1800 hours. That's when the radio guys swap duties."

"How do you know that?" asked Captain Brett.

Donovan shrugged. "I read the duty roster in the control room as we came down the ladder."

"Nicely done," Brett whispered. Then he leaned forward and carefully placed the first charge within the framework of the engine.

Donovan checked his watch again. They had fifteen minutes before the first charge would go. During that time, he needed to attach a second charge to the ballast tanks in the forward section. A two-fisted punch would ensure that the ship sank.

"Go on ahead," Brett said. "I'll meet you near the radio room in ten minutes."

Donovan backed out of the engine room. He passed through the enlisted galley where three men sat, including the chief engineer. Nodding quickly he kept going. His boots soon thudded against cross-sectioned steel deck plates. He was over the main ballast tanks.

Donovan knelt and pretended to tie his bootlaces. He eyeballed his surroundings, confirmed that only the three men were nearby, and reached into his jacket. He pulled out a prepared block of dynamite. It had been shaped to slip in between the deck plates and magnetically stick to the tanks.

"Did you fall, sir?" a voice asked from behind him. The chief engineer came up to Donovan.

Caught off guard, Donovan fumbled. The dynamite block slipped from his grasp and landed on the tank below him with a loud clank. But he hadn't had a chance to set the detonator.

Donovan turned and growled. "No, Sergeant!" he shouted. "Bootlaces do come undone. It is a matter of maintaining order, yes? Not unlike the conditions of your engine room. I have seen children's bedrooms that are cleaner. Don't think that Berlin won't hear about that in my report!"

"Yes, sir!" The engineer was flustered. "May I get you some coffee, sir? Our ship stores are from Brazil."

"Coffee?" Donovan repeated. He bent his head, as if thinking. He was glancing at his watch. Only five minutes before the engineering explosion erupted.

Captain Brett emerged from the room at the other end and entered the galley just as the engineer was scrambling for a cup and saucer. Eyes wide, he glanced at Donovan and then at the engineer.

Donovan shrugged slightly.

Finally, Brett stepped up, placed a hand on the big German's shoulder, and whispered in his ear. "The lieutenant seems a bit high-strung already. I don't think he needs the caffeine, do you?" Brett pulled a pack of cigarettes from his jacket. "Would you like to join me for a smoke instead, lieutenant? A bit of fresh air always does good, eh?"

"Certainly, Sergeant."

"Dunhill?" the engineer said as he caught a glimpse of Brett's cigarettes. "Where did you get those?"

Brett smiled. "Off the body of an Englander I killed in South Africa," he said.

"And what was a submarine engineer doing in South Africa?" asked the German.

The other men at the table rose. One of them rested a hand on his sidearm. They inched closer to the main hatchway between engineering and the command section. Donovan saw a ship's clock. Mere seconds now.

Brett lifted his chin and stepped back through the hatch. "What was I doing?" he said in English. "Killing Nazis."

None of the crew had a chance to respond as a massive explosion ripped through the engine room. A fireball barreled down the galley, engulfing the Nazis in a wall of flame.

Brett grabbed Donovan and yanked him through the hatch. He secured the metal door just as the fire was about to reach them. Donovan reached over and slapped the ALARM button on the wall. Red lights flashed in the darkness as Donovan and Brett scurried to the radio room.

Captain Lieutenant Peter Zschech was on the conning tower when the blast occurred. Smoke, men, and waves of heat rushed out the main hatches, vacating the ship. "What's happening?" he demanded as his first officer ran up to him.

"An explosion in engineering!" answered the first officer.

"Sound the evacuation!" ordered Captain Zschech. "Get all the men off the ship!"

Below them, the two commandos stormed into the radio room. An operator was placing the codebooks into a locker when he looked up and saw the two men. "What do you want?" he asked.

Brett knocked the German onto the deck with a strong right hook. Donovan grabbed the codebooks and stuffed them in his pack. "Let's go!" the lieutenant said.

They swiftly made their way to the front of the ship. Their plan was working. The entire sub was being evacuated. And luckily, when they reached the torpedo room, it was deserted.

After climbing the ladder and popping the hatch, Donovan and Brett emerged on the forward deck, near the bow of the submarine. Several men were topside, trying to board the same rowboat that had carried Brett and Donovan to the sub. Many of the crew were diving into the cold water. Others were already swimming away from the vessel toward their shipmates onshore.

At the docks, about thirty yards away from the Kübelwagen, a small five-ton truck sat unnoticed under a large tree. A big blue star was emblazoned on the side of the cargo tarp.

"There's our ride," Brett said.

"Swim?" Donovan asked.

Suddenly, the Brit's eyes went wide. Climbing out of the main hatch was the radio operator he had punched. The man, blood streaming from his broken nose, staggered to the top of the ladder and collapsed.

As the captain bent to help him, the operator waved his hands and tried to speak. He pointed toward the two Allies.

The German captain swiveled his head and locked eyes with Brett. "Halt!" he yelled. "Stop!"

Brett strapped the bag to his back and slapped Donovan on the shoulder. "Always loved the water," said the captain.

The two men plunged into the harbor and swam toward shore. The captain yelled at his first officer and pointed at the commandos swimming away from the sub.

The first officer slid down the main ladder and hit the main deck. He grabbed the nearest sailor by his shirt collar. Then he shoved him toward the twin 20-mm Flak gun. "Erschiessen!" he ordered. "Shoot!"

Donovan and Brett clambered onto shore. Donovan fell onto the grass, his wet uniform weighing him down.

Flak bullets chipped up all around them.

"Go, go, go!" Captain Brett screamed. He pulled a Walther from his bag.

Several yards ahead of them, the truck driver heard the gunfire. He quickly cranked the engine. Thick, gray smoke boiled from its tailpipe, and the truck slowly rolled forward.

On the dock, other German soldiers stood and stared in surprise as the two engineering experts from Berlin bolted across the road, chased by anti-aircraft fire.

"Hit them!" the first officer yelled at the German sailor.

"I'm just a cook, sir," the sailor explained as he yanked the charging handle and reloaded the weapon. He pulled the trigger. There was a click, then nothing.

"I think it's jammed, sir," the sailor said.

"Imbecile!" the first officer said. He yelled to the men on the dock. "Stop them! They're spies!"

Donovan and Brett ran for their lives as the skeleton crew of the U-505 began chasing them. The dock's security forces pulled out MP40s and started firing.

Brett and Donovan closed in on the moving truck. The back of the vehicle exploded to life. Whipping the flaps aside, four Danish Resistance members leaned out and aimed machine guns over the pair's heads, firing straight at the Nazis.

"Come on, Yankee!" one of the Resistance members yelled as Donovan neared the truck.

German bullets ricocheted off asphalt. The Resistance member grabbed Donovan and yanked him into the truck. Brett was right behind him. He put his hand out as Donovan braced himself on the tailgate.

"Brett, stop screwing around!" Donovan yelled.

Brett turned as he ran. He opened up on the Germans, dropping two of them. Then Brett spun back toward the truck and ran at full speed. He reached out his hand. He was inches from Donovan's straining fingers. The American was leaning dangerously far out of the truck toward his friend.

Immense pain stabbed through Brett's body. He stumbled as his left leg gave out on him. Blood flowed from his thigh and spattered darkly on the road. Donovan's hand moved farther and farther away as the truck moved off.

Donovan screamed over the gunfire, "We have to stop! He's been hit!"

An MP40 bullet flew past him and pierced a Resistance member's head. The Dane flopped back inside the truck, knocking into one of his comrades.

"If we stop, we all die!" another Dane yelled. The three fighters poured gunfire at the pursuing Nazis.

Brett limped behind them. "Keep going!" he shouted. He pulled the satchel with the codebooks from his back and held it in his hands.

"I won't leave you behind!" Donovan screamed.

"Catch!" said Brett. The Brit threw the bag and it sailed toward the back of the truck. Stretching as far as he could, Donovan leaned out, hands open.

The bag soared a foot away from Donovan's fingertips, fell to the road, and tumbled over and over. The stolen codebooks spilled from its open flap.

The throw was short.

Brett's face fell, defeated.

As he slowed his pace, Nazi bullets caught up with him. He pitched onto the road, face first. Blood pooled around his body.

"Ian," he whispered quietly.

And then he was gone.

A Resistance member held back the struggling Donovan as the truck barreled down the road and fled into the countryside.

Operation Deep Six was a failure. Though the mission hadn't yielded the results General Magruder and his peers had hoped for, however, it was discovered later that the explosive device set by Brett in the ship's main engine had been a success. The resulting blast had done its damage. When the U-505 returned to duty after months in dry-dock, her capacity for speed and escape maneuvers had dramatically declined.

Brett's sabotage yielded another positive result. The weakened sub was eventually captured. Fifty-eight German sailors were taken prisoner, and the Enigma codebooks were finally secured.

Donovan was sent back to Turkey and back to his desk. Although his mission did not succeed, he was commended and promoted to captain for his efforts.

***

Weeks later, Aaron Donovan stood on the doorstep of a quiet cottage on the outskirts of London, a small package in his hands. Nervously, he rapped on the door and waited. He tugged at the small wrinkles on his uniform.

After a short time, he heard the sound of a lock unbolting, and the door opened. Donovan hurriedly removed his cap and opened his mouth to speak, but stopped short. He looked down. In front of him stood a young boy, about seven years old, blond with blue eyes.

Donovan's mouth ran dry. He stood and stared, unable to speak, not sure what to say even if he could.

"Sir?" the boy said, gazing up at the tall American.

Donovan didn't answer. He was surprised at how much the young boy looked like his father.

"Ian, go back upstairs and play now," rang out a woman's voice. Elizabeth Brett came to the door. The boy stayed beside her, interested in the strange man.

"Is it about Nigel?" she asked softly, holding onto the door for support.

"My name is Captain Aaron Donovan, ma'am. I served with your husband."

She nodded. Though she stood strong, her eyes began to water, the breath caught in her throat.

Donovan held out the small package. "These were his. I just thought you should have them."

Elizabeth fumbled with the box. Inside were some of Brett's personal effects, including his brass trench lighter.

Elizabeth did not look up. "Were you with him?" she asked. "At the end?"

"Yes, ma'am, I had that honor," Donovan replied.

She picked up the small metal object. "It was Nigel's father's," she said. "He always wanted it to go to his son. But Ian's not going to be a soldier."

"No, ma'am," Donovan said. "I know he didn't want him to be."

Mrs. Brett stared at Donovan. "He told you that?"

"Yes, ma'am, he did."

She took a deep breath. "I think he would have wanted you to have this." She held out the lighter.

"I can't, ma'am," said Donovan.

"Please," she said. "You were his friend."

Donovan remembered when Brett had handed him the lighter in the Kübelwagen back in the Danish forest. "Hopefully, my son will never have to use it like we are," Brett had said.

Slowly, Donovan took it from her and placed it in his pocket. "Thank you," he said. "I know how much this meant to him."

"They told me he was killed in the line of duty," she said. "But they didn't tell me more than that." Tears began sliding down her cheeks. Her hands shook as she clutched the box.

"It was a top-secret mission," said Donovan. "Regulations don't allow them to reveal anything else. But—" He hesitated. "I think you deserve to know the truth. I think you deserve to know how he died."

Opening the door, the woman held out a hand.

"And I think you deserve to know how he lived," she said.

Taking her hand in his, Captain Aaron Donovan entered the Brett family home and closed the door behind him.

CAPTAIN
EVERETT DONOVAN

ORGANIZATION:
1st Marine Division, 3rd Battalion,
5th Marine
CONFLICT: KOREAN WAR
LOCATION: TOKTONG PASS, KOREA
MISSION: Scout an area known as the
Toktong Pass and provide security for UN and
U.S. military forces to advance through.

BLOOD BROTHERHOOOD

Sunlight.

Golden rays stabbed at the back of the man's brain. His eyes fluttered open. The world around him was hazy and out of focus. A muffled humming filled his ears, deafening his surroundings. He tried to sit up, but his head felt like he was balancing a bowling ball on his neck. His own breathing echoed in his skull.

Blinking, he tried to focus. The landscape surrounding him became clearer. Where was he? What was going on?

His eyes scanned over a filthy M2 carbine rifle still clutched in his hands. Its bolt was open and the ammo magazine was empty. His M1951 Cold Weather Uniform was caked in frozen mud and covered with snow. His hands, though dirty and bruised, were both still there and seemed to work okay. He used one of them to shield his pain-filled eyes from the sunbeams radiating down on him.

Getting to his knees, the soldier noticed something odd. He was standing in a medium-sized mortar crater. Fragments of the charred metal casings scattered about told that tale, but they were all covered in new snow. It was clear that whatever had happened hadn't been a recent event. He'd been unconscious for some time.

Desperately, the soldier tried to remember the events of the day. Every time he reached back into that part of his memory, all he could muster were flashes of white-hot light that made his skull ache. He shook the cobwebs from his head as his vision became locked-on and solid.

Time to figure out where I am, he thought.

Standing now, he looked over the edge of the earthy depression. What he saw made his blood run cold.

Blast craters. Spent ammo shells. Scorched earth. Smoldering trees. And between all of that lay the bodies of twenty dead United States Marines. Lifeless, they sank in a veil of freshly fallen snow.

Clearly, a battle had taken place here. And they had most certainly lost.

By the look of things, Captain Everett Donovan, 1st Marine Division, 3rd Battalion, 5th Marine Regiment, was lucky to be alive.

Coming out of the crater, he looked over what was left of his men. He was the captain in charge of these Marines, and they were just that—his. His team of Counterintelligence

Marines. His responsibility. And this? This was his failure. At least that's how he felt, though he knew that wasn't really true.

As he surveyed the bodies, tears welled in his swollen eyes. Donovan tried desperately to remember what had happened here, but nothing, not even a single image, came back to him. All he knew was that these men were gone, and somehow he'd survived.

Captain Donovan gnashed his teeth. He walked from one fallen Marine to the next. He removed their dog tags and searched the bodies for personal items like death letters that would be sent to loved ones in case they didn't make it home. He felt like a sick vulture as he knelt over them, rummaging through their pockets. A little part of him died every time he went through a fallen Marine's pouch.

Coming upon his radio operator, Donovan reached for the field radio, but it was punched full of bullet holes.

Well, that's not going to work, he thought.

Donovan looked at his watch. He estimated how long he'd been out. "Dang!" he said softly, examining the face. "I just got this fixed." The watch was cracked, just like it had been when his brother Michael gave it to him before he'd deployed.

"Dad would've wanted you to have this. It kept me safe in France, and I'm sure it'll do the same for you in Korea," he remembered his brother Mike saying. Though the glass was cracked, the gears were still going strong. The watch still kept perfect time.

"Just like a Donovan," Everett had replied with a grin.

"Like a Donovan, for sure," Mike had answered.

But no, he wasn't back home with his brother. He was stuck on the frozen tundra of the Chosin Reservoir in North Korea, fighting in conditions never faced by soldiers. He wondered how he'd even gotten here, especially after just fighting a war in the Pacific.

But the reasons didn't matter now as he squatted down and unfolded his map. Using his compass, he was able to zero his location and plot a route to the Marine Forward Observation Base. It was hard to know if they'd still be there. He didn't even know what day it was. Because of the freshly fallen flurries, and since extreme cold slowed body decomposition, checking bodies wasn't going to help figure out the date either.

It was 35 degrees below zero and getting colder as the sun started to dip in the sky. He needed to move. It was a five-hour trek to the base, but that'd turn into an entire day's journey, easily. Thanks to everything from long cliff drops to enemy land mines between him and the base—not to mention the entire Korean army—he'd have to take it slow. And since their Chinese allies had a reputation for not treating prisoners of war too kindly, the last thing he wanted was to be captured.

Suddenly, a light snow began to fall. Donovan slung his rifle over one shoulder and his bag of supplies over the other. After taking one last look at his men, he tilted his helmet to his fallen friends and set out across the frozen Toktong Pass.

Donovan had to stop himself from whistling as he continued his lonely trek through the snow. He tried to take his mind off the cold and the wetness, but melted snow soaked through his double-buckle combat boots and deep into his woolly socks. Whistling was a nervous habit he'd picked up at boot camp and one that'd landed him in trouble every time he was caught doing it. Every sergeant instructor that called him on it made him write essay after essay on "the merits of Noise Discipline and the reasons we have it."

The thought made him chuckle as he pressed through the trees, heading deeper into the Toktong Pass. Finally, he came to a small clearing in the forest and stopped. Crouching, he scanned the open grove. It looked like a small baseball field with tree lines on either side. The forest made great cover but would be a harder path to travel.

The forest was not impossible, but Captain Donovan was worried about land mines. The enemy would certainly have placed mines in there, knowing a person would fear the openness of the grove and would probably try to go around.

Looking at his map again, Donovan knew it was a guessing game, one he could go back and forth with for hours. Safe or not, it didn't matter. Straight through the open field was the fastest way, period.

Donovan looked up again and sighed. He unslung his weapon, chambered a round, and began slowly walking through the grove. The Marine was on high alert.

About fifteen yards in, Donovan noticed the true beauty of his surroundings.

Untouched snow blanketed everything in shades of white for as far as the eye could see. He marveled at how tree limbs were so used to the snowfall's weight, they dipped but didn't break. It was like something out of a Christmas painting.

As moments past, Donovan almost forgot he was in a combat situation. Almost.

Donovan's right shoulder suddenly jerked hard to the rear. His confusion was immediately replaced by intense pain that crashed over him. Waves of blood emerged from the new hole in his upper arm. It splattered red, contrasting sharply against the soft whiteness of snow blanketing the ground.

As his right arm flew backward, his rifle spun end over end out of his hand. Finally, it landed about five yards away from him. Donovan's feet corkscrewed under him, causing him to fall immediately to the ground with a loud thud.

Donovan had been shot by a sniper's bullet.

Gritting his teeth, he placed a hand on the wound. The bullet was lodged deep in his shoulder muscle. The wound wasn't life threatening yet, but blood loss and immediate infection would soon become a major factor. He scrambled for his sidearm, pulling it free from the leather holster. Then he looked at his M2 rifle, half buried in the snow.

Reaching for his rifle, Donovan yanked his hand back just in time as another silenced shot impacted the snow.

Out in the open, Captain Everett Donovan was in a bad spot. He knew he needed to get to cover fast, or he was dead. Donovan quickly got to his feet, eyed his entry point to cover, and began running toward the trees.

As he ran, shots exploded from his .45 pistol. Bullets pierced trees where he thought the sniper's location was, but he hit nothing.

As the tree line approached, he dove in, hit the ground with his good shoulder, and slid down a thirty-foot bank of frozen mud and snow. Finally sliding to a stop, Donovan shook off the pain. He raised his weapon. Nothing was in front of him. As he stood, the crunching of snow underfoot alerted him to someone behind.

With his pistol in the air, he stopped and opened his eyes wide. Pointed at his chest was the barrel of a Mosin-Nagant M91/30 sniper rifle with telescopic sight.

Holding onto the gun's hand grip was the biggest North Korean soldier Donovan had ever seen. He was five feet, ten inches tall, and 195 pounds of solid muscle. He was covered from head to toe in a light green uniform that had been bleached more white than green, thanks to the harsh elements. The jacket and pants were quilted for warmth, and Donovan wondered if this added to the man's bulk. Ammo pouches flapped open against the sniper's chest, revealing a well-stacked supply of lead. He wore a large bayonet on his belt.

This Korean was a killing machine, hands down.

Though his hand shook a bit, Donovan was able to hold his pistol in the air. The captain had never been in a situation like this before, and no amount of training could ever prep a Marine for a gun-to-gun, point-blank stalemate.

A moment passed before either of them did anything.

Donovan could feel the warm liquid flowing over his cold skin. Blood trickled down his arm, and the lightweight pistol began to grow heavy in his hand. As he fought to keep it in the air, Donovan grimaced slightly.

The Korean noticed.

And Donovan noticed the Korean noticing.

This made Donovan angry. He was a Marine and that meant he wasn't typically allowed to show weakness. But the events of the day were anything but typical.

"Funny, isn't it?" Donovan said with smile. "Two soldiers trained to kill the enemy at all costs, and neither one of us is willing to risk their own life to do it. Wonder if this is in a field manual somewhere?"

Donovan chuckled. Then he recoiled in pain as the jarring from his laughter caused his shoulder to flame up.

Slowly, Donovan retreated two paces, as did the Korean sniper. Donovan sat on a log, and the Korean sat on a broken tree stump. Neither one of them lowered their weapons.

Slumping on a tree, Donovan used his left hand to reach for his canteen. It wasn't there. He looked around, but he couldn't see it anywhere.

"Great. Not only am I gonna to die, I'm gonna die thirsty," Donovan said.

He cursed himself as he suddenly heard a sloshing in a metal receptacle in front of him. Looking up, he saw the Korean swigging a long drink of water from Donovan's own canteen.

"Son of a—! Where did you get that?" He groaned as pain filled his arm again. The world began getting darker. Blood loss was beginning to make him woozy.

"It was a stupid mistake, you know?" Donovan said.

The Korean soldier's eyes narrowed.

"It's the first thing they teach you," Donovan continued. "Keep moving under fire. Don't stop when the shooting starts—even if you're hit."

The Korean drank out of the metal canteen again. He appeared to listen to the American carry on. The way the sniper stared, the Korean almost seemed to understand Donovan's ranting.

"It's the hardest thing for a Marine to learn," Donovan explained. "Instinct makes you wanna hug the dirt, but something inside keeps yelling 'Move.' Finally you do, and you just hope it's in the right direction."

Glistening tears began to well up in his eyes. Donovan looked around, not sure what to do.

"This country is absolutely the most beautiful place I've ever seen," he said. "It's like a fairy-tale land or something, you know? I'm from Illinois. I've never seen anything like this. But what am I telling you for? You can't even understand me."

The Korean raised an eyebrow.

"But then it became a nightmare inferno," Donovan added. His eyes began to roll uncontrollably into the back of his head.

Shaking it off, he heard the sound of the Korean moving. Donovan tried to focus and looked up through blurry eyes to see the sniper almost on top of him.

As he approached, the Korean drew his large bayonet from its sheath. The setting sun glinted off of its metal blade as it cleared the leather carrier.

Though he tried to raise his gun, his arm wouldn't work, and Captain Donovan knew this was the end. And strangely, he was at peace with that reality.

Donovan smiled as he caught a glimpse of his brother's watch.

"Still going," he said weakly.

Then he passed out.

***

Twelve hours earlier, twenty Marines, each five meters apart, walked along the frozen tundra that was the Toktong Pass. Trees were sparse, and the cover of Mother Nature wasn't as dense as he would've liked. Captain Everett Donovan, 1st Marine Division, 3rd Battalion, 5th Marine Regiment, knew this was an area of operations for the Korean Army and was, unfortunately, where they needed to be.

He and his Counterintelligence Marines had been tasked with a scouting mission. They needed to make sure the coast was clear in this part of Korea so UN and U.S. Forces could advance through the area in the morning.

They had arrived. Now it was just a matter of reporting anything suspicious back to their commanders.

Gunnery Sergeant Helmsman, the platoon leader, broke from the others as they stopped. "Your orders, sir?" he asked his commanding officer.

Hills, snow, sparse trees, large boulders, and a total lack of cover meant they were out in the open and could be seen for miles. Helmsman didn't like it.

An older, gruff Marine, Helmsman had been with Donovan in the Pacific during World War II when Donovan was still a first lieutenant. They had history—in combat and out.

On the other side of the Marines, about three miles to the north, lay a small range of mountains that encircled the entire Chosin Basin.

Nodding, Donovan motioned toward the mountains. "The 59th is getting ready to trek through here tomorrow, Gunny," he said. "They're supposed to meet up with the 89th and the 79th. We're all going to meet at the Chosin Reservoir. If Inchon was the beginning, hopefully, the battle at Chosin will be the ending."

The Gunny shook his head disapprovingly. "Home by Christmas, sir?" he asked.

Smiling, Donovan looked over at the old devil dog. "That upset you, Gunny?" he asked.

"A Marine's place is on the battlefield, not curled up in front of a fireplace like a pussycat, sir," the Gunny barked back at his commanding officer.

Donovan nodded and replied, "I agree."

A light snow began to fall as several of the Marines pulled on gloves and pushed up woolen scarves.

"Not like the Philippines, is it, Gunny?" Donovan said.

"Cold, hot, damp, dry—I don't care, long as my rifle don't freeze shut," Helmsman said, gritting his teeth. "I don't care much about where the fighting's done, as long as I'm the one left standing when it's over."

Helmsman wasn't one for officers. Most of them didn't know their elbows from Jeep tires, but Donovan was different. The captain listened and cared about his men. And in turn, they respected Donovan.

Helmsman sighed. "It's a bad plan, sir," he said.

Looking over at his gunny, Donovan frowned. "Okay, Gunny, what's eating you?" he asked.

"The Chinese 9th Army is gathering in the towns of Yudami-ni and Sinhung-ni," said Helmsman. "If they push toward Hagaru-ri, they could trap the UN forces on the road between Hagaru-ri and Hungnam."

"Blocking them and the 1st Marines into the Reservoir," added Donovan. "No chance of escape."

"No sir," said Helmsman.

This made Donovan smile. "Then it's a good thing Marines don't retreat, isn't it, Gunny?" he asked.

The Gunnery Sergeant smiled. "Yes, sir, it is indeed."

"Break 'em into their fire teams," said Donovan. "I want a report from each on them. If the 9th Chinese is out there, I want to know about it sooner than later."

A flash of light, a tremendous earth shaking, and two Marines were killed in an explosion. Secondary explosions rang out as Chinese mortars began raining down on the Marines. They scattered, diving for cover wherever they could.

"That soon enough for ya, sir?!" the Gunny scoffed as he racked the action on his M2 rifle and opened fire.

From over the ridgeline to the north, what looked to be about eighty Chinese and North Korean Army soldiers attacked without question or pause. Expertly, the Marines fired back. Lifeless, Chinese and Korean troops dropped to the dirt. Those who didn't continued to advance as small puffs of smoke appeared in the cliff side.

"INCOMING!" Gunny screamed as he reached up and threw the captain under the cover of a nearby boulder.

As Donovan rose, he fired his weapon. In the distance, he saw two Chinese soldiers fall, his aim true. Donovan reached down to help Helmsman up. "Come on, Gunny, we need to—" he began. But the gunny was dead, having taken most of the explosive force himself to save his captain.

Donovan took pause, shaken, but an old saying ran through his head: "Concentrate on the ones you can save, and mourn the dead later."

Stick and move, he thought as mortars and rifle fire rained down on them from the entrenched position.

Yelling at his squad leaders, Donovan ordered his men to spread out. "Return fire!" he commanded. "Ya can't hurt 'em if ya don't hit 'em!"

They were outnumbered, and with the Chinese above firing down on them, the Marines wouldn't last long at this location. They needed some air support from the Navy's F9F Panthers and fast.

Ducking and weaving, and with bullets chasing him all the way, Donovan ran to his radio operator.

"Get me—" he began, but Donovan noticed the young radio operator was dead as well. He grabbed the radio handset and turned away from the gruesome sight. Keying the handset, Donovan yelled into it. "Crossbow 15, this is Cobra 22. I have U.S. casualties—break—we are covered by mortar and small arms fire at two niner romeo."

A series of pops came as Donovan ducked, sparks flying all around him. The radio was destroyed in a hail of gunfire.

"No!" he yelled. He threw the handset to the ground and fired at the enemy. Two more Koreans fell.

The Koreans and Chinese pushed forward, their numbers multiplying.

"They're comin' for us, sir!" one of his Marines screamed over to Donovan.

"Then at least we know where they are, and they won't get away!" Donovan yelled back. Brass shell casings flipped from his weapon.

His words and his confidence echoed throughout the ranks. He brought a loud "Hoorah" from the men, energized for the fight. The Marines fought hard, but the odds were just too great. Marines crumpled to the deck as Donovan ordered the rest of them to pull back.

One of the Marines was hit square in the chest, and Donovan came to his aid. Placing a hand over the wound, he tried to stop the bleeding, but it came too quickly.

"Corpsman!" Donovan yelled. He looked for the squad's medic, but he was nowhere to be found.

"Don't worry, Sullivan, you'll be outta here soon," Donovan said, grabbing the kid's hand.

But the young Marine knew better. "Sir?" he said. "Please let my pa know... I... I fought with honor."

Donovan agreed. "Like a warrior, son."

And with that, the young Marine was gone. His hand went limp, and Donovan rested it on the young man's chest. Then he picked up his weapon.

Donovan crouched and placed bloody hands next to his mouth, amplifying his words. "Split up and get to Rally Point Alpha!" he commanded the troops.

They divided and began to move in groups. One squad covered the other as they backed out the way they came. But the dropping explosives kept coming, and finally, they completely overwhelmed the Marines.

Looking up, Donovan saw his own fate approaching as a mortar came right for him. He dove out of the way, but the concussion of the explosion blew him through the air. Helmet first, the captain was smashed against a rock and rolled off. His limp body settled in a mortar crater, unconscious.

***

Donovan's eyes popped open.

Frantic and scared, he wasn't even sure where he was. The returning memories of the last day still lingered in his mind.

Eyes darting, he observed that night had fallen. A small flickering campfire was burning, lighting up the surrounding trees. As he glanced upward, he saw the Korean sniper standing over him like an angel of death, the bayonet still in his hands.

But now, it was covered in blood.

Panic filled Donovan as he screamed and lashed out like a child. He flailed as he rose, kicking the sniper away from him. Reaching down, Donovan snatched up his .45 pistol, cocked it, and moved forward.

The Korean hit the deck as Donovan came down on him hard, slamming a boot into his chest. Donovan pulled up his .45 pistol and aimed at the Korean's forehead. The sniper dropped his knife and raised his hands.

"*Anio! Anio!*" the Korean pleaded.

As it fell, the knife hit a small metal drinking cup on the ground. The liquid splashed up and onto Donovan's boots, which drew Donovan's attention downward. He breathed heavily, just about to pull the trigger.

Swirling with the water from the cup was a large amount of blood, but it's what was swimming in the sticky liquid that gave Donovan pause. A small lead ball, mushroomed and misshapen, was covered in a layer of deep red blood.

A bullet.

Donovan looked over at his arm. A fresh field dressing, white and sterile, had been applied to his shoulder. The sniper had used his bayonet to dig the slug out and then bandaged him up.

Donovan's head began swimming. Confused, he felt like he was going to pass out. Backing away, Donovan lifted his boot from the sniper's chest, but still covered the Korean with his weapon. He glanced between his shoulder and the defenseless enemy still on the ground, pleading for his life.

At that instant, it hit him. The Korean had saved his life.

Emotions swirled in Donovan like a massive tornado.

Why? he wondered. *Why did he do it? Was it a trick? Am I to be taken captive for interrogation? Or is he genuine?*

These questions, coupled with the flashes of returning memories of the previous day's events, finally broke the brave young Marine to his core. He slumped onto the log again.

Tears flooded down his cheeks. Donovan sucked air, letting out small moans as he wept.

He'd seen his share of death and destruction during the Pacific campaign. He'd never see another like it in his lifetime. It was nothing like he'd seen today, not even Iwo Jima.

"They...they came at us like a tidal wave," Donovan said. "They didn't stop. And those men..."The captain stopped. His head slightly cocked to the side as his eyes went wide. "Those boys," he corrected himself, "fought like warriors. But we didn't have a chance. When the mortars started pounding us from above, Gunny shoved me under cover. He—" Donovan stopped again. His body trembled uncontrollably.

Very slowly, the Korean sat up, leaned against the log he once sat on, and listened to Donovan cry in the darkness. The small fire reflected off of his face. Donovan's tears glistened in its golden glow. His eyes settled into a distant stare.

"They couldn't move, they were pinned down by rifle fire. We lost two in the first attack," Donovan said. "The looks on their faces. There was nothing I could do. Eighteen Marines, laying there, one on top of another. Crying. Yelling. Burning. And you know what? You know the worst part? What I will never forgive myself for?"

Through the tears, Donovan looked up at the Korean. "I'm alive, and they're not," he said. Eyelids shut, the captain tried to squeeze out the pain. "Why? Why didn't you just let me die?"

The sound of sloshing made his eyes open. He saw his canteen before him.

Compassion filled the Korean's eyes. The sniper offered some water to the wounded American.

"Because I make choice. Choice for life. Not just for you," the Korean said softly.

Eyes wide, Donovan looked at him in shock. "You speak English?" he exclaimed.

The Korean held up his thumb and forefinger. "Little bit," he said, offering up the canteen again.

Slowly, Donovan dropped his pistol and took the canteen. He sipped off the top. The swallow went down hard as the water stuck in his scratchy, dry throat. After handing it back, Donovan grinned as the Korean took a sip.

A moment passed. The two men, sworn to kill each other, sat sharing a canteen. In their own little section of the world, the war seemed far behind them.

"I don't know why you fixed me up," Donovan said. "I mean, you did shoot me, but maybe it's true. It's easy to kill the faceless enemy, but when you get up close and personal, it changes all the rules."

The Korean stood and walked over to a tree at the far end of the encampment. He leaned against the frozen bark. Looking out into the meadow, the enemy pondered the American, his words, and these last two hours of his life. He understood exactly what the captain was saying.

"Okay, look…the way I figure it, we've both got somethin' to get home to. I'm going to back outta here the way I came in," said Donovan as he rose.

"I don't want to kill you," Donovan continued, "so let's just call it a truce and walk away, eh? Sound good?" He outstretched his hand, the gesture of a friendly handshake.

The sniper turned to him, but he suddenly looked angered. A cocked-back hand in the air, he let his fist fly forward like a rocket and clobbered Donovan in the jaw.

The punch sent Donovan reeling to the ground with a resounding thud of flesh and equipment. The Korean stepped over him, retrieved the Colt, and grabbed Donovan by the collar. In an instant, he hoisted Donovan up by the coat and slammed him into a tree. Pistol in the American's face, he angrily barked at him in Korean.

Completely confused by this behavior, Donovan eyed the sniper wildly. Behind him, an entire platoon of Korean soldiers suddenly marched out of the woods, their guns in the air.

The platoon commander walked over to the sniper. The sniper saluted with a head nod, his hands busy holding the American prisoner. This nod signaled that the other man was a commanding officer.

The commander began asking the sniper questions that Donovan, of course, couldn't understand. But he got the gist of the conversation. The sniper punctuated his answers by slamming Donovan against the tree.

Finally the commanding officer smiled and snapped his fingers, and one of the other Koreans stepped forward and handed the sniper an entrenching tool.

The platoon leader narrowed his eyes, looked at the American, waved good-bye. He rallied his troops, and they moved out.

The sniper grabbed Donovan by the collar and led him deeper into the woods, in the opposite direction of the Korean patrol. He yelled the entire time. Gun to his back, Donovan trekked through the trees. The sniper led him by the scruff of the neck.

"So that's it, huh? Orders? I didn't get through to you at all, did I?" Donovan said, continuing his death march.

The Korean sniper was suddenly, and eerily, silent. His face was emotionless, like he was a robot now, the perfect killing machine.

Moments later, they reached the clearing where he had shot Donovan. After letting go of Donovan's collar, the sniper threw the encased entrenching tool at Donovan's feet. He motioned for Donovan to pick it up.

Angered, Donovan spit on the ground. "No way!" he shouted. "You can kill me if you want, but there is no way I'm diggin' my own grave!"

But the Korean shrugged. He waved at the tool, motioning with the .45 pistol for Donovan to pick up the canvas-cased shovel again. And again, Donovan refused.

Frustrated, the Korean squatted down and grabbed the tool, flipping it over. Another case was attached to its back. This one, a map carrier with compass, was strapped to the entrenching tool. It was a common practice to carry two pieces of equipment as one.

The Korean offered it to Donovan, and the captain slowly began to catch on to what was happening.

The sniper was letting him go.

Pointing at the map, the sniper traced a small path leading back to the Toktong Pass—a better route to where the Americans had been amassing troops.

The sniper pointed to the mountains. "You go!"

As Donovan turned to run, he stopped and reached down into his webbing. Throwing something to the Korean, he nodded and said, "Here..."

Reaching out, the Korean caught Donovan's canteen.

"...and thanks," Donovan added.

The Korean smiled and waved him off. "Go!"

Giving a slight salute, the Marine turned and booked it across the clearing. As he ran, the Korean raised the Colt into the air, taking aim at Donovan's back. He closed his eyes as he pulled the trigger. Two shots rang out as the Korean sniper stood, alone in the meadow. His pistol, aimed high, smoked in the cool night air.

He looked out over the clearing to see Captain Donovan, United States Marine Corps, disappearing into the trees.

Snow began to fall as the sniper made his way back into his camp. Exiting the cover of the trees, he nodded hellos to the guards who recognized him as he made for his tent. His rifle hung over his shoulder. The American's canteen was tucked secretly into his shirt.

The night was especially cold, even for a Korean winter, and several of the soldiers had lit fires in fifty-gallon drums. The flames licked at the biting wind. Soldiers stood in packs, warming themselves over the fire as the sniper approached.

His comrades welcomed him back to camp, calling him a hero to the people for what he had done to the Marine. Of course, he played along. He knew a firing squad would be his fate if what he had done was even suspected by the others.

As he warmed his hands over the fire, his commanding officer slapped him on the back. "Excellent work, Jung-woo!" he said, smiling from ear to ear.

The sniper bowed his head, not making eye contact with his commander. "Thank you, sir," he replied.

"Come! All of you!" the commander said, waving everyone to follow. "It has been a long day and much has changed since you were on your patrols." He entered the tent.

Inside was dark, lit only by the five red-lens lanterns that sat on the work spaces edging the walls of the tent.

This was the platoon's operations center.

Plastic-covered maps hung on the walls and various pieces of communications equipment flanked the large table in the center of the space. On it sat an image of the entire Chosin Reservoir, with several locations circled in red.

"Because of the American attack today, we doubled our mine-placing efforts!" said the commander. "I am happy to announce the entire Toktong Pass has been fortified with a perimeter that not even a foot soldier could pass through!"

Confused, the sniper eyed the map. That was exactly the area he had sent the American into, not ten minutes earlier.

"In the morning, the PVA 20th and 27th Corps will launch multiple attacks and ambushes along the road between the Chosin Reservoir and Koto-ri. We will be a part of that attack," the commander said proudly.

The soldiers cheered and waved fists in the air. The chance to strike against the invading Americans made them all proud to be fighting for what they believed in. All but the sniper.

Sadly, the sniper left the celebrating soldiers behind as he quietly snuck out of the tent. The bitter cold slapped his face as he walked alone, the cheers of the men fading out behind him.

He stopped as he came to the edge of the trees, and leaned against one of them. Above, the moon was full. Its glowing face stared back at him.

The sniper mouthed a quiet prayer for the American he had unknowingly put into harm's way. The sudden sound of snow crunching behind him made him turn.

"What's the matter, Jung-woo?" the commander asked as he approached the sniper.

The sniper sighed. "Tomorrow will be the beginning of a bloodbath, sir..." he said, continuing to gaze at the moon with concern.

The commander smiled. "Yes," he said. "And it will be the beginning of a glorious victory for the North."

"Even a single dead man is anything but glorious," the sniper replied. "It's wisdom, compassion, and courage that are the moral qualities of men."

"Bah!" the commander said. "We must fight to protect our way of life—to continue as a unified people—or all will be lost. The politics of this war are very hard to understand."

"Confucius tells us life is very simple, sir, but it is we who insist on making it complicated," the sniper said.

The commander put a hand on the sniper's shoulder. "Confucius understood what it was to be a soldier," he said. "We truly appreciate life, because only soldiers know how quickly it could be taken away."

The sniper nodded. "But Confucius wasn't a soldier, and nothing in today's world is simple."

"Then why? Why do we do these immoral things? Murder people over land, or a different way of thinking than our own?" the commander asked.

"Because we're soldiers and when you're a soldier, it isn't murder, it's your duty. All war is immoral but if you let that bother you, you're not a good soldier," he replied.

They both gazed up at the moon.

Finally, the commander looked at his sniper. "We've known one another for a very long time, Jung-woo. What's really troubling you?"

"It's…" Stopping, Jung-woo looked at the ground and chuckled a bit. "It's complicated."

The distinct sound of an exploding mine rang out in the distance. Puzzled, the commander's gaze shot up to the horizon. He saw the small puff of gray smoke, backlit by the heavenly glow of the moon, rolling into the air.

The commander glanced from the smoke to his man and back again. But all became immediately clear as the Korean sniper removed Donovan's canteen from his belt and offered it to the commander.

"Drink, sir?" the sniper asked.

Eyes narrowing, the commander took the sniper by the arm. "Traitor!" he said angrily as he knocked the canteen out of his hand. The water spilled out, pooling up on the ground.

"Guards!" the commander yelled. Behind them, two armed soldiers appeared and took the sniper into custody.

"You will pay for what you have done!" the commander yelled.

The sniper cocked an eyebrow at his commanding officer, tears welling up in his eyes.

"We all will, sir. But that debt will not be settled by man," he said as the guards dragged him away.

PRIVATE FIRST CLASS
TONY DONOVAN

ORGANIZATION:
U.S. Army, 249th Engineer Battalion

CONFLICT: KOREAN WAR

LOCATION: 38th PARALLEL, KOREA

MISSION: When a U.S. Army cargo
plane crashes behind enemy lines,
soldiers must repair a vehicle from the
wreckage and quickly evacuate to safety.

DAMAGE CONTROL

"Richards? Donovan? Anyone?!"

The words echoed through the cabin of a mangled C-119 cargo plane, but they seemed to get swallowed up by choking flames. Twenty-four-year-old 2nd Lieutenant Drew Polaski stumbled around the interior of the downed aircraft. He coughed and waved thick smoke from his face. He squinted through the toxic black clouds, searching for his crew.

The main fuselage of the plane was tipped on its side. Sunlight streaked in from the gouges in its metal hull, life-taking wounds in the belly of the aircraft.

The battalion had crashed behind enemy lines—fifty kilometers from the Demilitarized Zone in the mountains of South Korea. It was a miracle anyone was alive. The pilot and copilot were gone, but they'd done their jobs. They'd landed the limping plane the best they could.

As the C-119 dropped from the skies, the ten men of 249th Engineer Battalion had braced for impact. But when the plane dipped, the chains strapping down their cargo had snapped like twine. The twin Willys Jeeps, five pallets of supplies, and various engineering equipment had danced wildly around the cabin. So had the men. The soldiers were tossed around the plane like out-of-control Ping-Pong balls.

That is, until the plane had slammed into the side of a mountain. The entire front end of the aircraft had collapsed in like an accordion. Several of the soldiers hadn't survive the tremendous impact. The bodies of the dead were now scattered throughout the cargo bay.

Lieutenant Polaski continued searching through the wreckage for any signs of life. "Richards? Donovan?" he hollered again. This time, however, the sound of stirring metal caught his attention.

"I'm—I'm okay, sir," came a voice from under the spare hood of a Jeep. It was Private First Class Tony Donovan. Slowly, the soldier pushed the hood aside and stood. He wiped debris off his green coverall uniform.

"You're bleeding," noted Polaski.

A trickle of crimson blood ran down Donovan's forehead. "I'm okay, sir," said the private. "But thanks." He wiped the wound with his hand and smeared the blood on his trousers.

Private Donovan looked at the carnage around the plane. "How many, sir?" he asked his lieutenant.

Polaski bowed his head. "You're the first person I've found alive—" he began.

"But not the last!" called a voice from outside the cargo bay. "Out here!"

Donovan and Polaski rushed toward the shout. The tail section of the plane had been sheared clean off. In the middle of the wreckage, they spotted the massive silhouette of a man, slumped to his knees.

"Sarge!" Donovan called out, scrambling toward him.

Standing with Sergeant Richards were three other soldiers: Corporal DeLori, Corporal Reed, and Corporal Soares. They all looked worse for wear, but they were alive. That's all that mattered now.

"You okay, boys?" asked Lieutenant Polaski, following Donovan toward his troops.

"Not bad, considering the situation," answered Corporal Reed. He was still chewing one of his trademark sticks of Beeman's gum.

"How you doing, kid?" Sergeant Richards asked Donovan.

Donovan was shaken, but he didn't want to show it. "Well," replied Donovan, "any landing you can walk away from is a good one, right, Sarge?"

"Ha!" Richards laughed. "The kid's got a sense of humor, boys. Now I know I'm dead!"

The other men chuckled. But Donovan could tell right away that Lieutenant Polaski didn't see any humor in their situation. Jeep parts, tires, weapons, ammunition, and broken cases of rations littered the area.

"First order of business," the lieutenant said, "is setting up a perimeter—nothing, nobody gets through. DeLori, you take Corporal Soares and recon out twenty meters. Make sure we're alone in this jungle."

Corporal Reed and Soares glanced at one another.

"Yes, sir," DeLori finally mumbled. He looked back at the lieutenant with concern. "But—"

"But what, Corporal?" Polaski asked.

"We don't have any weapons, sir," replied DeLori. "What if we run into enemy patrols?"

Polaski cursed himself. "Hadn't thought of that, Corporal."

"Sir? If I may," Richards began.

The lieutenant glanced over. "Go ahead, Corporal."

"One of the cargo crates had weapons and ammo inside," added Richards. "DeLori, Reed, and Soares, spread out and find it. Distribute one rifle and three magazines to each man. Give the lieutenant a sidearm if you find one. Understood?"

"Yes, Sergeant," said the other men. The corporals quickly spread out, clambering through the wreckage to find any precious cargo.

"Don't worry, sir," Richards told the lieutenant. "They'll find it. But what's the plan after they do?"

"We wait," replied Lieutenant Polaski.

"For what, sir?" asked Sergeant Richards.

"Rescue," said the lieutenant. "The pilot radioed our position as we went down. It's standard operating procedure."

"No offense, sir," Richards began, "but the Korean Army's got this area locked down pretty tight. If we just sit here—with no operational radio—the rescue choppers might not spot us in time."

"Those are my orders, Sergeant!" Polaski snapped. "We wait for rescue! Got it?"

Richards clammed up tight. Private Donovan knew the sergeant wasn't happy to be shut down in front of an underling.

Fortunately, Donovan knew Richards was right. It was dangerous to remain out here—even with weapons. The local Korean Army patrols would come searching for survivors. Richards knew that, and so did Donovan.

Standing nearby, Donovan piped up nervously, hoping to break some of the tension between his two superiors. "It's gonna get dark soon, sir," he said. "I'd like to volunteer to schedule out a fire-watch rotation."

"Donovan's right," said Richards. "It's a good bet the enemy knows we're here. We should be on alert."

Lieutenant Polaski looked at the sergeant and nodded. "Get to it," he commanded. Then he turned and stumbled off toward the fallen aircraft's cockpit.

With the lieutenant out of earshot, Sergeant Richards shook his head. "This isn't good," he mumbled.

"What, Sarge?" Donovan asked, overhearing.

"The KPA's gonna be on us like a swarm of bees," Richards replied with a sigh. "That's the problem with new LTs. They wanna to do everything by the book, but they ain't got no common sense!"

Donovan chuckled and then looked at the horizon. The sun dipped behind the trees in the distance, casting a golden glow over the pitted aluminum hull of the downed aircraft.

"It's going to be a long night," said Sergeant Richards. "Get that fire-watch rotation set. Schedule two-hour rotations between each man, and don't take the first watch. Give it to Corporal Reed. Right now, you and me will take grave detail. Our boys don't deserve to rot in the sun like this."

Donovan slowly glanced around at the wreckage. He'd almost forgotten about the boys who hadn't made it. The ones whose bodies now littered the ground like trash. "Okay," the private finally replied.

Richards leaned in, placed a hand on Donovan's shoulder, and looked him in the eyes. "Mourn them later," said the sergeant. "Because if I'm right, this will all get really bad before it gets any better."

***

Soon, the curtain of night had fallen. With no stars or moonlight, the area was blacker than a coal mine. The tree line was thirty yards from where the wreckage had scattered at the foot of the mountain. A large rip in the forest made by the aircraft's crash landing was bound to bring the enemy in.

South Korea was a beautiful, mountainous country, filled with dense forests and rolling hills covered with whitecaps of snow and ice. It was also a harsh country, and the environment had taken its toll on everyone involved in the war. Extreme conditions and below-zero temperatures were killing American soldiers by the hundreds. The weather also made transporting gear and supplies to the front lines incredibly difficult.

But Private First Class Tony Donovan knew that, like his cousin Everett fighting at the nearby Chosin Reservoir, he must survive.

Looking south while he kept watch, Private Donovan tried to picture Everett, a U.S. Marine Corps Captain. He wondered if their platoon's failure to transport supplies would directly impact his cousin's situation. Donovan prayed this wasn't the case. However, he knew that every soldier counted on these resupply drops, and he felt a sense of personal failure.

Donovan shook it off. He scanned the tree line for any sign of human contact. He knew that it was only a matter of time before the Korean People's Army came to investigate the fire in the hills.

Meanwhile, a small man-made campfire crackled inside the dimpled tail section of the plane. A piece of the wing, propped over the opening of the compartment, created a makeshift door that covered the fire from outside view. Smoke floated skyward through a monstrous hole ripped in the ceiling from when they had crashed.

Huddled around a small map and compass, the corporals of the 249th Engineer Battalion assessed their situation with

Sergeant Richards. Outside, PFC Donovan continued walking the perimeter, his new M1 Garand gripped in his hands.

"We're about fifty miles from the border, as far as I can tell," said Corporal DeLori, pointing at the map.

Reed rose, his arms crossed across his chest. "Ah, this is just stupid, Sergeant Richards," he grumbled. "Pilot's message or not, HQ's not going to send out a rescue team for us."

"Yeah, we're not important enough," said DeLori. "The Chosin Reservoir is about to explode, and they don't have time to look for five guys lost in the mountains. They're just gonna write us off. The new LT's gonna get us all killed, waiting out here like fish in a barrel."

"Hey! Like it or not, the man's in charge," said Sergeant Richards. "He says left, we go left. It's that simple. There's a chain of command for a reason, for just this type of emergency."

But not everyone agreed.

Soares stood and paced. His cold, moist breath clouded the air. "That's baloney, Sarge, and you know it!" he finally exclaimed. "You were there in Europe, and you know most of these officers don't have a clue what they're doing."

"What do you suggest, Soares?" Sergeant Richards asked. "Should we disobey orders? Run off and leave the lieutenant here alone? Where are we gonna go?"

Richards glanced around at the other men. "You all trust me, right?" he asked.

The corporals nodded.

"Then trust me now," Richards said. "I'm not going to let anyone get killed out here. If rescue doesn't come by zero-seven, I'll reassess with the LT, but until then—"

"Intruder!" Donovan called from outside. The sudden sound of metal on metal echoed in the cabin, like rocks being hurled against the outer hull. Then came the sound of igniting gunpowder.

"Move!" Richards shouted.

The soldiers jumped to their feet, rifles in hand. Richards kicked down the makeshift door, and he and the others emerged from the plane, weapons up and ready for a fight.

Private Donovan crouched behind a pallet of machine parts, taking cover from the enemy fire. "Contact at one o'clock," he yelled.

Quick flashes lit up the foliage in front of him. Two North Korean soldiers sliced through the tree line, taking potshots at the U.S. soldiers.

"Weapons free!" Richards commanded.

All five men spread out and returned fire at a rapid pace. Bullets flew through the air from both sides as leaves rustled in front of them. The Koreans were on the move.

"They're up," DeLori shouted. He began to move in a crouch, flanking left.

"Covering fire!" Private Donovan yelled. The other soldiers concentrated their shots in a center mass, around the flashes in the trees.

Breaking cover, DeLori headed toward the tree line, bullets chasing him and chipping up earth all the way. He took shelter behind a piece of metal debris from the crash site. Then he returned fire with his M1911 pistol. One of the two Koreans fell to the ground, racked by bullets. Stuffing from his cold-weather uniform sprinkled the air around him. The second Korean bolted, disappearing into the night. As he ran, the soldier pointed his 7.62mm Tokarev rifle behind him. He pulled the trigger wildly, trying his best to cover his escape.

The U.S. soldiers hit the dirt as the shots whizzed through the sky. Corporal DeLori jerked backward. He'd been hit. The slug flung him to the dirt in a heartbeat.

Richards rose and waved his hand in the air, giving the signal to stop shooting. "Cease fire! Cease fire!" the sergeant shouted. "He's gone. Save your ammo, boys!"

"I'm hit!" yelled DeLori. He writhed on the ground in pain, clutching his shoulder.

Behind them, Lieutenant Polaski emerged from the main body of the crumpled wreck. He skinned his M1911 pistol from his holster and held it high in the air. "What have we got, Sergeant?" he asked, his eyes nervously scanning the darkness.

"Oh, man," mumbled Corporal Reed. He shook his head and reloaded his M1 Garand.

"Afraid you missed the party, sir," replied Sergeant Richards. He looked at his young leader with disgust. "But DeLori didn't. He's been hit."

Lieutenant Polaski turned his attention to Donovan. "You were on watch, Private!" the lieutenant shouted. "Why didn't you call?"

"I did, sir," Donovan said.

"Well, I didn't hear it, Private," said the lieutenant.

"We all heard him, sir," said Sergeant Richards. "We ran out ASAP."

Kneeling at DeLori's side, Corporal Reed tried to calm his friend. "You're going to be okay, DeLori. Just relax," he said, peeling the blood-soaked uniform from the corporal's wound.

Reed looked down at the bullet hole and grimaced. The bullet had entered DeLori's shoulder, bounced off of his collarbone, and exited his back—but not before piercing his right lung.

Corporal Reed turned to Sergeant Richards and shook his head slowly.

Richards looked at his commanding officer. "Sir—"

"Don't, Sergeant! We're not abandoning this crash site!" Polaski ordered. He stepped up to Richards, locking eyes with the much larger sergeant. Leathery and tan, with his strong jaw covered in stubble, Richards stood fast and calm. The younger, fresh-faced lieutenant stared at him with authority.

Sensing the tension, Donovan moved in. "With all due respect, sir, this is a losing battle," he said. "That was a Korean scouting party. Since we didn't kill both of them, that other KPA soldier is on his way to report what happened here."

"How do you know that, Private?" Polaski asked, keeping his eyes on Richards.

"That's what I'd do," Donovan answered.

Quietly, Polaski addressed Richards directly. "This is all your doing, trying to breed dissent in the ranks."

"You're new, Lieutenant," said the sergeant. "I get that. It's been a hard day. But if you ever question my loyalty again, I'll knock you on your butt. Sir."

Eyes wavering, Lieutenant Polaski broke off the staring match. He looked briefly over at his men. They were all scared and tired, and none of them knew what to do next.

"Look, sir," the sergeant said quietly. "These boys are engineers, not combat personnel. If the KPA comes down on us in numbers, we're gonna get slaughtered."

The lieutenant removed his helmet and wiped a hand over his crew-cut head. After a second, his shoulders dropped and his stance became less defensive. "We're not going to get far on foot, Sergeant," he said, "and both of the vehicles are smashed. What do you suggest?"

Richards shook his head. Donovan knew he didn't know what to say. But Donovan did. He'd been thinking about it since they landed. He decided to speak up.

"Actually, sir," Donovan said, "we could salvage what we can from the site. You know, take parts from each of the vehicles, and see if we can get one running."

"No," Polaski said. "SOP says we wait."

Sergeant Richards eyed his commanding officer. "Sir, at least let them try," Richards said. "It'll keep morale up while we wait. If they can make it work, it'll be a good plan B."

Polaski was visibly frustrated. Donovan could tell he was tired of this conversation. The lieutenant waved them off.

"Fine, but just as a backup plan," said the lieutenant. "And on their own time."

Richards nodded over to Donovan.

The private took off running. For the first time since the crash, he felt a sense of purpose.

***

It had been the longest night of Donovan's life. He and Corporal Reed had performed surgery on the dying Jeep, transplanting one metal organ for another. The men had taken turns between walking the perimeter and turning a wrench.

Now, the sun was beginning to rise over the scene of destruction. No one was sure if they'd get a heartbeat out of their Frankensteined Jeep.

"Hand me the crescent wrench, will you?" Corporal Reed asked Donovan.

Donovan found the tool and slapped it into Reed's hand.

"Shine some light in here," Reed ordered.

Donovan produced a brass WWI-era trench lighter and sparked the flint.

"Nice antique," Reed said with a smile. "Where'd that come from?"

"My cousin," Donovan answered. "He got this in WWII from a British soldier. Said it always kept him out of harm's way on his missions during the war. He gave it to me to keep me safe."

Reed nodded and smiled again, this time, sadly. "Guess its lucky powers don't extend to other wars."

"We ain't dead yet, Reed!" Sergeant Richards's voice boomed into the plane's main fuselage. He strode inside, rifle slung over his shoulder. "How's it coming?" he asked the men.

Standing and wiping grease from his hands, Private Donovan looked at the Jeep and shrugged. "They're pretty tough crackers, Sarge," he said. "Both engine cases took anti-aircraft fire when we were shot down. We've spent the night replacing headers, pistons, and filling any holes with spit and gum."

"Will she run?" asked Richards bluntly.

"Yeah," answered Donovan. "I think."

"How long until we can blow this Popsicle stand?" Richards asked.

"I dunno." Donovan scratched his head. "Another hour, give or take."

"Good," said Richards.

"Wait, Sarge," Donovan said. "I'm just saying she'll start. I have no idea how long she'll run."

"It's gonna have to do, Private," said Richards.

***

"That's good to hear," said Polaski after Sergeant Richards had given him the news. The lieutenant looked into the sky and then back down at his watch.

Adjusting the rifle sling on his shoulder, Richards looked at his CO and shook his head. "Sir, it's been over twenty-four hours," he said. "If KPA was coming, they'd been here by now."

"Maybe so," Polaski said.

"But DeLori," continued Richards, "he ain't gonna last much longer. And I know he'd rather go out fighting than just sitting around and dying."

The lieutenant rose. "You're right," he said. "I'm sorry I didn't listen to you sooner, Richards. Let's get the men to gather up what they can. We're getting out of here—"

A sound like a small thunderclap echoed through the air. Red liquid, thick as syrup, sprayed from the lieutenant's neck and splattered Richards' face.

Eyes wide in surprise, Lieutenant Polaski gasped for breath. He stuck a hand out to support himself. But he missed the Sergeant's shoulder. Then he crumpled, his knees buckling below him.

"Lieutenant!" Richards screamed, dropping to the side of his commanding officer.

Private Donovan came running from inside the wreck. He stumbled, fell, and then crawled to the pair.

Small bubbles popped from Polaski's mouth. The blood in his throat made a gurgling sound every time he tried to breath.

"What happened—?!" But Donovan stopped short as round after round of enemy gunfire ripped up the dirt around them.

"G-g-go!" Polaski managed to spit out.

With a quivering hand, the LT tried to pull his pistol from its holster, but he just wasn't strong enough.

Sergeant Richards pulled the gun from its cowhide sheath. Then he handed the .45-caliber pistol to his CO and nodded.

Polaski held the weapon in the air and squeezed the trigger. A few rounds ripped into the trees. It was a last-ditch effort at covering fire as Donovan and Richards ran for the fuselage, bullets hunting them all the way.

About fifty yards away from the crash site, an entire platoon of thirty-five KPA soldiers was spread out in the bushes. They quickly advanced on the five remaining American soldiers. The enemies moved swiftly, their triggers depressed and empty brass casings spitting out of their weapons' ejection ports. Bullets zinged and whipped through the forest. They peppered the crash site and found their way into the fallen body of Lieutenant Polaski—a cruel end to his tour of duty.

The corporals rushed toward the opening of the fuselage. At the same time, Donovan and Richards came storming in, bullets bird-dogging their footsteps.

"What's happening?" asked Corporal Reed, nervously popping a bubble of gum against his lips.

Suddenly, shots splattered the hull from all sides. The soldiers ducked and dropped to the deck.

"Answer your question?" Donovan muttered. He crawled, belly to the ground, toward their Jeep.

Sergeant Richards looked up and finally saw his men's handiwork. Several pieces of the plane's hull had been bolted to the exterior of the Jeep. With the makeshift armor screwed onto the body, the vehicle looked like a heavy-duty M1 Scout car. "I'm impressed, boys," said the sergeant.

Then the sergeant looked down at the wounded DeLori. "Is he ready?" Richards asked Corporal Soares.

The corporal finished putting the last of the morphine into DeLori's arm and nodded.

Smiling, Richards leaned in and spoke to DeLori softly. "We're leaving, kid," he said.

DeLori understood. The men lifted him onto the standby stretcher made from shirts and piping from the plane.

"And the LT?" asked DeLori quietly as they placed him in the rear quarter of the transport and strapped him in with the seatbelts. Everyone froze at the question.

"He's gonna be watching our backs, pal," Donovan lied. "Just rest and hang on."

Bouncing into the front passenger seat, Soares yelled, "Shotgun!"

"You know that means you're in charge of protecting the driver, right, kid?" Richards said smugly.

Glancing around nervously, Corporal Soares jumped out and let Richards have the front seat.

"Right, you better take it then," the corporal mumbled.

Sergeant Richards sat, placed a foot on the A-frame for support, and loaded his rifle. Donovan slid into the driver's seat beside him. The private placed a hand on the ignition key and said a silent prayer.

He turned the key. Nothing happened.

Letting out an exasperated sigh, Donovan sprang from his seat, popped open the hood, and looked inside. "Reed, you and Soares cover the door!" he ordered.

After running to the front of the plane, the two men crouched behind old crates. They opened fire, trying their best to buy some time. Outside, the KPA were advancing on the tree line, firing blindly at the site. They were a mere twenty yards away from them.

Under the Jeep's hood, Donovan quickly spotted the problem. A small amount of fuel was leaking from the fuel line. It had been hit by a stray bullet. Donovan looked around the cabin for something to fix it with, but there wasn't anything in sight. "All I need is some tape, or something sticky—"

The idea hit him like a land mine.

"Reed!" yelled Donovan.

Popping shots from his M1 Garand, Reed didn't look back. "Little busy, Private!" he shouted.

"You got a stick of that Beeman's gum?" Donovan yelled to the corporal.

"Just the one in my mouth!" Reed yelled back.

"That'll do," Donovan said.

"But it's my last piece!" Reed protested.

Suddenly, a Korean soldier sprang up in front of Reed. The enemy thrust his bayoneted rifle toward the corporal's chest.

A sudden shot came from inside the fuselage. It struck the Korean and sent him reeling backward.

Sergeant Richards racked the action on his rife and glared at Reed. "Give him the gum!" Richards ordered.

Corporal Reed reached into his mouth and threw Donovan his chewed-up bubble gum. The young private caught the sticky wad. He spread it out like taffy, carefully wrapped it around the fuel line, and pressed it tightly.

Donovan jumped back into the Jeep and tried the key again. This time, thick clouds of black smoke belched from the exhaust pipe as the Jeep tried to return to life. Chugging and rattling, the Jeep turned over.

"Punch it, Donovan!" Richards ordered.

Donovan slipped the Jeep into first gear. As it rolled out, Corporals Reed and Soares leaped into the back.

After exploding from the fuselage, the up-armored Jeep sped down the embankment. It took heavy fire from the KPA as they advanced out of the trees.

Two Koreans tried to rush the Jeep, but Reed hammered out. He butt-stroked him across the face with his rifle as they drove off. Bullets ricocheted off the makeshift armor, but the cleverness of the American soldiers had paid off.

Trees whipped by them at fifty miles per hour. Eventually, the men felt they were far enough away from the KPA troops to finally relax a bit.

"Where the heck am I going, Sarge?" Donovan yelled over to Richards.

The sergeant was urgently trying to read a small map in his lap as they bounced along the road. "We're headin' south, and that's good!" he said. "We were—"

Bullets zipped in through the windshield. Glass shattered into the front seat and cut the sergeant under his left eye. Appearing like a ghost, a Chinese carrier truck squealed onto the road. It kicked up dirt and rocks as it slid in behind them, gaining quickly.

"Vehicle from the rear!" yelped Corporal Reed.

He and Corporal Soares pulled their triggers as quickly as they could. Meanwhile, Donovan slammed on the gas, doing his best to keep the Jeep ahead of the truck.

But the enemy troops kept advancing.

"Hang on, boys!" Donovan shouted.

Reed and Soares held DeLori tight.

Donovan turned the wheel again, but this time, the Jeep's nose was suddenly pointing down a steep decline. They were headed straight down the side of a dirt-covered mountain.

"This is gonna get rough!" said the private.

The Jeep jerked like a bucking bronco as it descended over the lip of the mountain. The men desperately tried to hang on.

In the back, Corporal DeLori opened his eyes and smiled. "We at Coney Island, Pete?" he joked.

With one hand clutching his helmet and the other holding his wounded friend, Soares couldn't help but laugh. "Almost there, pal!" he said.

Finally, the Jeep settled at the bottom of the hill and headed south again, leaving the befuddled KPA troops at the top of the hill. Or so they thought.

A massive explosion rocked the ground to the right of the Jeep, almost flipping them over. A shower of dirt and rocks rained from the sky. It sprinkled down on the soldiers as a tremendous crater appeared in the ground.

All the men turned to see a metal behemoth crashing through the forest, collapsing trees like toothpicks. An IS-3 Iosif Stalin tank crashed onto the road behind them.

It fired again.

Weaving right, the Jeep just missed the tank shell as it impacted with the ground. The tank began to give chase as it roared off after them.

"Faster, Donovan! Faster!" Richards yelled as he, Soares, and Reed fired at the tank.

Their aim was true, but the shots were useless. They bounced right off the tank's armored hull.

Donovan swerved the vehicle, doing what he could to avoid being targeted. But the action just made it harder for his men to take accurate shots.

From the top of the tank, the main gun hatch popped open and a KPA soldier emerged. Taking the machine gun handles in his hand, he opened up on the Jeep. Thick, chunky shots echoed out of the anti-aircraft gun. Rounds sped through the air, impacting the ground all around the Jeep. Though it had a slower rate of fire than most machine guns, the projectiles still did their jobs. They pierced the Jeep's hull.

Inside, the U.S. soldiers yo-yoed back and forth, doing everything to hang on for dear life.

"Take that sucker out, Sergeant!" Private Donovan yelled. He ducked as hot lead zipped past his ears at subsonic speeds.

Sergeant Richards placed his elbow on his knee and the barrel of his weapon against his seat back. He steadied the weapon the best he could.

Then he squeezed the trigger.

Suddenly, the tank gunner's head snapped back like it'd been hit with a baseball bat. However, the enemy soldier's fingers were wrapped tightly around the firing mechanism. As the KPA soldier slumped over his weapon, bullets flew wildly through the air.

One lucky shot from the dead soldier's gun blew out the Jeep's front tire.

The Jeep's rear wheels left the road, kicked up, and flipped over into the air. Rolling left, the Jeep flew for a few feet, but crashed down hard on its side and ground to a halt on the heavy dirt road.

Behind them, the tank stopped and, for an instant, all was quiet. The men in the Jeep had survived, but looked worse for wear. Donovan, still behind the wheel, looked over and saw Reed. The corporal was lying behind the cover of the wreck, about three yards away. Richards was in the passenger seat, and DeLori was straight up, still strapped into his stretcher.

Corporal Soares' legs were pinned between the road and the Jeep, and he was unconscious.

"Another crash landing," Reed grumbled. He rose slowly and grabbed his rifle.

Springing to life, Richards grabbed Soares' rifle and shoved it into Donovan's hands.

"We ain't done yet," Richards said. He covered the backside of the Jeep. Donovan crouched over the hood, peeking around the front quarter of the vehicle.

A sudden mechanical clicking sound filled the air. The enemy tank's turret swung in their direction. Its D25-T 122-mm gun ratcheted down toward its target.

Swallowing hard, Richards knew none of them would ever see home again. "Gents," the sergeant said, looking around at his men. "It was a pleasure serving with you." He smiled and racked the action on his M1 Garand.

Reed smiled back and nodded. "We all gotta go sometime."

"Let's make it count," Donovan said. He grinned and readied his weapon.

"Fire—!" Richards ordered.

Just then, the tank exploded. A ball of orange flame and searing heat rose into the air. Fragments of the KPA tank's armor plating flew through the sky, slamming against the underside of the Jeep and causing the men to duck for cover.

For an instant, all three men shared a look of disbelief.

"How?" Donovan asked, but Richards shook his head.

Corporal Reed glanced behind him, and instantly a smile blasted across his face. "Look!" he yelled, pointing to their rear.

Into the clearing, an M4 Sherman tank was rolling up on their position. Its 75-mm gun was smoking.

Looking at Donovan and Reed, Sergeant Richards smiled. "Boys, we're going home," he said.

***

The men were evacuated to a M.A.S.H. unit about fifty kilometers from the 38th Parallel. The area separated the two warring factions of North and South Korea from one another, and it was far enough from the fighting that they could relax.

Rumors of the soldiers' acts of heroism quickly spread through the mobile hospital. The stories filled everyone with inspiration. The men started to believe that the brutal war could be won with American know-how and determination.

But not everyone felt that way. A lone figure sat in the quad between all the M.A.S.H. unit tents. He looked into the air as the medical helicopters roared off into the distance.

"This stinks," Corporal Soares said. He sat in a wheelchair, staring at the blue skies.

"Ah, you'll be up and playin' basketball again in no time," Richards said, strolling up behind him. On his face, there was a small bandage where the doctors had stitched up his cut.

"And DeLori?" asked Soares.

"It's too close to tell right now," said Donovan to Reed.

"We're just lucky anyone got out alive," complained Soares. "Lieutenant Polaski almost got us all killed."

"Actually, the LT was right," said Richards. He pulled a pair of mud-caked dog tags from his pocket and handed them to Corporal Soares.

Soared growled. "Whose are these?" he asked.

"Polaski's," said the sergeant. "That armored patrol was actually out looking for us."

"Really?" asked Reed.

"Yeah," Richards said. "Seems the pilot's Mayday got through. They would've rescued us in an hour."

"Problem with being in charge is having to make decisions that impact other people's lives," Richards said. "Polaski played it by the book, and he was right. They did come for us."

"But if we had stayed and waited, how many of us would have been alive by the time they'd gotten there?" Soares asked.

"Try not to judge him too harshly, Pete," Donovan said. He placed a hand on his friend's shoulder. "Polaski only did what he thought was right."

"And in this life, boys, that's all any of us can ever do," Richards said.

LIEUTENANT
VERNER DONOVAN

ORGANIZATION:
VF-96 squadron, U.S. Navy
CONFLICT: VIETNAM WAR
LOCATION: ĐÔNG XOÀI, VIETNAM
MISSION: When the Marine Recon unit
Razor Two takes heavy fire on the
ground in Vietnam, the VF-96 "Fighting Falcons"
squadron must provide air support.

FIGHTING PHANTOMS

Lieutenant Verner "Candy Man" Donovan unwrapped silver foil from around a tear-dropped bit of chocolate. He popped it in his mouth. Then he turned and laughed at his radar intercept officer, who really didn't like being in the Navy.

"I'm just sayin' it's a job, not an adventure," said Lieutenant Bobby "Blam" Hassleback. The young recruit shifted in the back seat, doing his best not to ruin the latest copy of the *Amazing Illusions* comic clutched in his hands. "Especially given the cramped quarters."

Blam was right. The cockpit of an F-4 Phantom II was cramped. They were a two-man flight crew, pilot and RIO, strapped into the front nose cone of a 60,000-pound fighter jet. While in their cockpits, the men that flew in the VF-96 "Fighting Falcons" squadron from the deck of the CVA-64 USS *Constellation* aircraft carrier were gods among men.

They were masters of flying these two-man wrecking machines. They commanded jets that carried 5000-pound bombs, thousands of rounds of ammunition, and air-to-air missiles. The Fighting Falcons attacked targets and disappeared into the clouds before the enemy even knew what hit them.

They were phantoms.

Donovan's F-4 was parked in a Ready-Five formation on the carrier's deck. It was locked onto the steam-driven catapult and primed for launch. He could take off and be in the sky, ready for battle, in less than five minutes. The anticipation was nerve-racking, and the men did what they could to avoid focusing on it. In this case, Blam read comics, and "Candy Man" Donovan ate chocolates.

"It's not like you were drafted, Blam, you volunteered for this," Donovan said, licking caramel off his teeth.

"Yeah, for college credit," Blam replied. "Not for getting my butt shot out of the sky!"

Blam chuckled as Donovan's eyes glanced back at him from the jet's small rearview mirror. They were strapped so tightly into their ejection seats it was difficult for Donovan to turn around and glare at him.

"And what did you think a radio intercept officer was, anyway?" Donovan asked.

"You know, a radar man!" said Blam. "A guy that sits in an air-conditioned room all day and says, 'Look out, plane to your left!'"

Donovan shook his head. He adjusted the ear pad on his flight helmet. Each of their helmets were standard-issue gear.

However, pilots and their crew were encouraged to decorate them any way they saw fit. Donovan's was painted chocolate brown with gold and purple stripes. Swirls of gold reflective tape adorned the sides. Above his visor control knob, in small white press-on letters, CANDY MAN was taped. This was Donovan's call sign, a nickname given to him because of his love for sweet treats.

Blam's helmet, on the other hand, was bright yellow with white starbursts. His call sign, BLAM, was also taped above his visor. Many people thought he had gotten the name because he was an amazing fighter, but it was really given to him because of his love for comic books. He always had one with him.

Radio traffic filled their headsets as the control tower communicated with the daily patrols over the coastline of Vietnam. Donovan tried to focus on the chatter, but Blam kept on yapping.

"But of course, you want to be here." Blam smiled.

Donovan chewed on another caramel-centered morsel. "That is correct, my friend," he began. "I come from a long—"

"A long line of military men," Blam finished. "I know all that, but don't you get sick of all the rules?"

Donovan scoffed and looked at his RIO in the mirror. Crumpling up the handful of foil into a small wad, Donovan threw it over his shoulder and hit Blam square in the face.

"Dude!" Blam said with a laugh. The foil rolled off his chin and into his flight suit.

"Splash one!" Donovan yelled, but his joke was cut short.

"Hush!" the lieutenant ordered.

A broken transmission came through the airwaves. "Marine recon unit Razor Two requesting close air support," crackled out of Donovan's headset. Both men quickly became all business.

"That's our cue," Donovan said. He flipped on the F-4 Phantom's electrical systems. A smooth hum settled over the interior of the aircraft. Blam folded up his comic and shoved it into his hip cargo pocket.

Outside the jet, the scene around them transformed as the deck of the carrier came alive. Men in different colored vests and headgear swarmed the blacktop. They waved wild arm signals in the air like rabid third-base coaches.

High above the scene, looking down on the carrier deck from a tall tower, the commander of the air group spoke into a microphone. Air traffic controllers read radar screens. They made sure the skies above the carrier were cleared.

Maps of the area were hung on boards marking the enemy positions. The carrier was anchored 50 miles off the shores of Vietnam.

Below, blast shields rose out of the deck right behind the main engines of the two jets that readied for take off. In the cockpit, Blam and Candy Man sat, illuminated by the orange glow of their instruments as the catapult officer got into position on the far side of the ship.

With the engines firing full-throttle, the catapult officer put a hand to his helmet and saluted. Donovan returned the salute from the cockpit, planted his helmet firmly on the headrest, and grabbed the handhold on the right of the canopy.

Twisting his body, the catapult officer dropped to the carrier deck on one knee. He pointed forward, signaling for the launch petty officer to hit the button and fire the catapult. Flame, steam, and a loud howl from the jet's engines signaled the beginning of the mission. Donovan's F-4 Phantom shot toward the shores of Vietnam.

Once in the air, the F-4 climbed as Donovan pulled the throttle back, disengaging the afterburners. In a flash, the pilot and his RIO were over land. They streaked toward the jungles of Dong Xoài. A full moon cast an eerie hue over the tropical wilderness.

"Home Plate Zero One, this is Iron Hand One Three Niner. We are feet dry, over," Donovan radioed.

"Roger, Iron Hand One Three Niner," the controller replied. "One more minute on that heading to the turn point, over. Coordinates Gulf, four-five-two, over."

"Roger that, Home Plate Zero One," Donovan replied.

"What have we got?" asked Blam. He swept the skies for any sign of enemy contacts from the jet's back seat.

"Looks like Marine Recon patrol, Razor Two, stumbled into a Vietcong training camp," said Donovan. "They need some help from above."

"Jarheads," Blam joked. He flipped on his radar screen. "They never look where they're going. I mean come on, it's 1968, man! Don't those boys know how to read a map yet?"

"Roger that," answered Donovan. He reached down and locked a silver tab into his helmet, securing the rubber oxygen mask to his face. His eyes became narrow and confident as the 24-year-old gripped the flight stick.

The F-4 streaked through the air like lightning, and then turned sharply left, leveling its wings.

Suddenly, an energy wave appeared on Blam's scope. "I got enemy radar," he said. "It's sweeping for a target."

On the ground, hidden by a layer of camouflage netting, a radar dish cycled back and forth. It scanned the skies for enemy contacts. Soon, it had found one.

"Activate jamming signal!" Donovan ordered.

Pressing a series of switches, Blam activated the plane's electronic countermeasures. These devices transmitted jamming signals on all frequencies, making their plane invisible to radar.

"Jamming!" he yelled as he eyed the screen intently.

"Razor Two, this is Iron Hand One Three Niner," Donovan radioed. "Request you pop yellow smoke to mark your position. We don't want Kentucky-Fried Marines for chow tonight, over."

Pops, bangs, and explosions filled his headset. "Roger that, Iron Hand!" the Marine radio operator finally answered back.

"Them Vietcong are advancing north on our position. Attack against the tree line—a hundred yards northeast of our smoke!"

Whoa! Donovan thought. *That's pretty close to our friends. Those Marines must be in serious trouble.*

"Have you got it?" Donovan asked Blam as his head surveyed the tree line in front of them.

Blam smiled as a plume of yellow, wispy smoke began to rise up in the distance. "Contact," Blam answered back. "Yellow smoke bearing two-seven-five at eleven o'clock low."

Donovan pushed the stick in that direction. "Tally ho, stepping into target," he said. "Thirty seconds."

The plane's nose dipped as Donovan pressed the stick forward. For his attack run, he lined up with the trees that whipped by him at 600 miles per hour. With a target that close, the lower he could get, the better accuracy he'd have when he released his bombs.

Blam coordinated the computer with the area the Marines had designated as the target. "We're locked," he called out to Donovan. "Fifteen seconds to target. Arm the explosives."

Leaning in, Donovan flipped the ARM switch on his weapons panel. "Pickles are hot," he called out.

As the target approached, they could finally see the dull glare of the fighting. Hot tracer fire from both sides filled the skies between the trees like lasers in the night. Small-arms explosions rocked the jungle floor, sending showers of mud and grime skyward.

Secretly, in that instance, Donovan was thankful that he was relatively safe in his multi-million-dollar armored jet fighter. He wasn't on the ground, slinging lead at the enemy, hip-deep in jungle mud like his father and grandfather had been decades before him.

Brought back to the fight, Donovan shook off the daydream as the beeps signaled his target was locked.

"Drop 'em and climb, Candy Man!" Blam ordered from the back seat.

Donovan pushed the button on the control stick. Clicks echoed out underneath the plane. The safety pistons released, allowing the bombs to float away from the belly of the aircraft.

As the Mark 82 bombs fell, their tail fins splayed open, allowing a controlled descent to the ground. Spinning lazily, the bombs dropped toward their target and, in a few quick seconds, ignited the jungle in a rainbow of yellows and reds.

"Razor Two, Iron Hand, good strike?" Donovan radioed to the Marines on the ground.

A tense moment passed as silence filled the cockpit.

"Roger that, Iron Hand! Good shooting!" finally crackled through the static. "We all owe you a cold one when we get back to the real world!"

Donovan nodded proudly. "Roger that," he said. "Razor Two, keep your—"

But a shrieking alarm rang out, cutting him off. On his instrumentation panel, a red MISSILE warning alarm flashed.

"Blam, what is it?" Donovan yelled.

"An air-to-air missile!" he replied.

"Where?!" Donovan asked, his eyes scanning the horizon.

A short-range, air-to-air missile lit up the night sky. It launched through the trees, did a midair spin, and accelerated right for them.

"I've got it!" Donovan said. He pushed the control stick hard to the left. As the plane swept away from the deadly missile, Donovan pressed a button marked DISP on his right throttle control.

Two small discharge tubes suddenly opened above the jet's wing flaps. They sprayed a cloud of debris into the air. Donovan smiled. The thick cloud of metal filings would, hopefully, look bigger on the missile's radar than his plane did. The missile would swing toward the decoy, not the jet.

"Chaff's away!" Donovan said as he kicked in the throttle.

Behind, the missile came dead for them. Then suddenly, it turned and headed for the cloud of raining debris. Seconds later, the shock wave from the exploding missile rippled through the air.

"Yeah!" Donovan yelled, but a slight beeping from the back seat caught his attention. *Now what?* he thought.

"Multiple contacts! Multiple contacts!" Blam shouted from the rear seat.

"Huh?" Donovan asked.

"We've got company," his RIO replied.

Without hesitating, Lieutenant "Candy Man" Donovan slammed the F-4 Phantom's control stick to the right, dodging a Vympel K-13 air-to-air missile. The explosive narrowly missed the belly of his aircraft. He began to wonder what had gotten him into this situation in the first place. But there wasn't time to dwell on those thoughts now.

Donovan was in the zone. Hyper-focused thoughts drifted, and reflex and instinct took over. The screaming enemy missile, however, brought him quickly back to reality.

Two MiG-21 aircraft had entered their airspace on radar. In seconds, the skies looked like an angry hornet's nest.

At 12,000 feet above the ground, the three planes swarmed one another, each going in different directions. As they fought for position, the jets snapped past one another like ends of wild bullwhips.

Underneath them, the earth spun. The horizon appeared and disappeared from view of the pilots time and time again.

Extreme g-forces flattened them against their seats. Candy Man strained his neck to track the enemy jets that streaked past at Mach One, more than 700 miles per hour.

"Where are they?" Donovan yelled back to Blam. He slammed the control stick to the right, causing them both to roll to the starboard side of the cockpit.

With each hard turn, Candy Man and Blam grunted. Their specialized g-suits kept blood from rushing to their brains. Still, the flyers fought to keep themselves from passing out.

"Ungh!" Donovan strained. "MiG One is moving away from us, MiG Two…" He looked around, attempting to see behind them. "…is on our right and coming fast!"

Hot lead and glowing tracers flew through the night sky. The MiG Two opened up and fired from behind, its cannon blazing. Donovan jerked the stick left and the F-4 took an astonishing turn. The second MiG roared past them, arcing wide, missing them completely.

Donovan didn't slow as he powered the throttle down, dropped his flaps, and rolled the Phantom hard right. Then he thumbed the weapons selector on his control stick to GUNS.

The jet swung around, coming in right behind the MiG's tail. On his electronic display, an orange diamond appeared around the enemy jet. "Target locked" signals echoed in the darkness of the cockpit.

Donovan pulled the trigger. On the nose of the plane, the night illuminated as the Vulcan cannon exploded to life. It blasted molten-hot lead at the MiG.

"Come on!" Donovan grunted, adjusting his elevation. He strained to pull the bullets into the MiG's position.

After a moment, the metal slugs dug deeply into the enemy jet, causing irreparable damage to its systems. Smoke belched from the holes in its hull. Fuel and hydraulic fluid ignited in the sky. With a resounding blast, the MiG exploded, sending a hail of flaming debris and scorched metal toward the ground below.

There was no time for celebration. The F-4 Phantom was caught in a hail of cannon fire from the first MiG. The enemy had circled back around, sweeping down from above them.

Donovan broke hard. He dove deep as both jets now streaked across the sky, low to the deck, skimming the treetops of the jungle. Pulling up and slamming the throttle into overdrive, Donovan engaged the afterburners and went completely vertical. He shot the Phantom jet up straight and hard, aiming for the moon.

"Faster, he's coming around!" screamed Blam as he looked at his scope. Vapor trails came off the missile as the MiG launched and followed the F-4 into the night sky.

Donovan hit the DISP button again. This time, the cloud of debris didn't work. The explosive crashed through the metal decoy cloud and kept on coming like a bloodhound on their scent. It would be on them in a matter of seconds.

In the cockpit, Donovan grasped the metal handle and yanked it up with all his might. Spinning left, the MiG's missile didn't even twitch. It flew straight up the Phantom's tailpipe. The canopy flew off and away from the aircraft. The ejection seat rockets engaged, blasting Donovan and Blam out of the plane as the missile detonated.

The U.S. fighter jet exploded in midair. Heat and flames licked at the heels of the Navy F-4 Phantom. The only remnant of the magnificent machine rained down and scattered across the jungle in a streaking pile of burning rubble.

Clicking off and falling away, the ejection seats plummeted to the earth. Their chutes popped open, catching enough air, thankfully, to deploy their main chutes. They fluttered open with a sudden pop.

In the wink of an eye, Candy Man and Blam found themselves floating earth-bound on silken cushions of air. They were headed toward certain danger. Behind enemy lines.

***

Slowly, the metal top-slide on the .45 pistol glided back. The ammo magazine spring located in the handgrip released slightly, pushing a single round into the chamber. Quietly, Donovan pushed the metal slide forward again, locking the bullet into the barrel, ready to be fired.

Donovan looked down at the pistol in his gloved hand and grimaced. This was a last resort. He hadn't fired a handgun since his yearly qualification time, and that was almost ten months ago.

"She's easier to operate than an airplane, fighter puke!" he remembered his USMC marksmanship instructor telling him and the other pilots. "Just point and squeeze!" They stood on the firing line squeezing triggers while aiming at paper targets across an empty field at Camp Pendleton, California.

And of course, Donovan had seen every John Wayne movie on the planet. He was pretty sure he'd be okay. Well, at close range, anyway. But these suckers were loud and would have every Vietcong patrol in a mile radius on top of him.

Donovan looked around the darkened jungle, letting his eyes adjust to the new environment. He was still a bit shaken. Ejecting out of a perfectly good aircraft will do that to you. But he'd gotten lucky. His descent had taken him right into a dip between two massive tree canopies, allowing him to completely miss the thick bamboo and branches on the way down. Still, he was worried about his radio officer.

Donovan stopped. He held his breath and listened for enemy patrols. *Nothing but the sounds of a typical jungle oasis,* he thought, crouching next to a tree. Reaching down, he unbuckled his parachute and unzipped his g-suit, allowing them to fall to the ground.

With a deep breath, Donovan moved into the trees. About forty yards away from his landing position, Donovan saw Blam lying on the ground. He was wrapped up in his own parachute cords and not moving.

Eyes wide in fear, Donovan crouched and moved quickly. He made as little noise as possible in the dense underbrush as he moved toward his friend.

"Blam!" Donovan whispered as reached his injured side.

"Uh, man," Blam moaned weakly. "Who taught you to fly?"

Donovan smiled. He dropped to a knee and holstered his pistol. "Your momma," the lieutenant shot back with a grin.

Kneeling next to Blam, Donovan began unwrapping the thick nylon cord from around his friend's torso. Then he looked down and saw Blam's leg.

Splitting the fireproof fibers of the flight suit, a shard of bamboo stuck straight through the RIO's left knee. It had entered from the rear, piercing through the front of the kneecap bone.

"Oh man, this is bad," Donovan whispered. The lieutenant pulled a small folding pocket knife from his left cargo pocket.

Blam groaned again. "Why do you think I'm still on my back?" he answered painfully.

Cutting the material, Donovan was shocked to see blood pour onto the ground. It had been pooling up inside Blam's suit since he landed. From what he could tell, the bamboo had slit an artery.

He's lost a lot of blood, Donovan thought to himself. The lieutenant tried to remember his basic battlefield lifesaving techniques. Stop the bleeding, he recalled and began cutting away another nylon cord. Then he looped the cord around Blam's leg and twisted it tight with a small branch.

"Blam, I'm going to tourniquet your—" started Donovan, looking over at Blam. The RIO's eyes dipped lazily and closed. Donovan reached up and slapped him hard across the cheek. "Hey, you with me?"

"Yeah, yeah...I'm back," Blam mumbled back as Donovan kept twisting the stick, which cut off the blood flow to the open wound. "Thanks, Doctor Kildare."

Blam rested his head back against the tree. Then he unzipped his left breast pocket.

Donovan reached in and removed his short-range VHF radio. "Home Plate Zero One, this is Iron Hand One Three Niner, come in, over," he said, pressing the TALK button on the handheld radio.

After what felt like a lifetime of waiting, a reply finally came. "One Three Niner, this is Zero One, go ahead, over," the voice said.

Donovan let a grin slip from his lips as he continued transmitting. "Iron Hand is down," he reported. "I repeat, Iron Hand is down. One severely wounded and in immediate need of a medical evac, over."

"Roger that, One Three Niner," said the radio operator. "Check your chart."

Unzipping one of his many pockets, Donovan removed his map of the area. He unfolded it on his leg as he crouched. It was dark, but the slight moon shining through the trees allowed him enough light to read. "Roger, go," he said.

"Need you to reposition to two-niner-romeo, delta echo, 1689 2957," the radio operator relayed.

The directions confused Donovan. He traced the lines on his map with his fingers. Those map coordinates were nowhere near their position. "Confirm last?" he asked. "That's more than nine kilometers from here!"

"Confirmed," replied the RO. "Enemy resistance is too hot for helicopter recovery in your location. We need you to relocate to rally point at those coordinates within three hours."

Donovan checked his watch.

"If you're late, we'll be gone—" the RO continued. But a rustling nearby followed by softened shouts made Donovan quickly switch off his radio.

"What is it?" Blam said weakly.

Donovan silently shushed him with a finger. He skinned his .45 pistol and cocked back the hammer.

Getting on his stomach, Donovan belly-crawled up to a log. He pulled a pair of binoculars from his right breast pocket, adjusted the focus, and took a look. Ahead of them, about a hundred yards out, fifteen Vietcong soldiers glowed in the moonlight. Each of them carried an AK-47 and a cache of other deadly weapons. They were in a tactical wedge formation, like an arrowhead slicing through the jungle. They combed the area for something important.

"Vietcong," he said to his injured partner. "Standard search pattern. They're looking for us. We need to move."

Blam shook his head in pain. "No, you do," he said. "I'll just slow you down."

"What? No!" Donovan nearly shouted. "I am not leaving you here!" Donovan bent over to grab Blam. He started to pick him up in a fireman's carry, but the RIO slapped Donovan's hand away.

"Look," Blam said loudly, getting Donovan's attention. "We both know I'm not gonna make it to the pick up, especially not by five o'clock."

Donovan looked down at Blam's injury. He knew Blam was right. There was no way he'd make it another three hours, even if they weren't on the run. Two hours was the absolute amount of time you could tourniquet a limb. It had already been over forty minutes, but he didn't want to face this fact. He didn't want to admit that his best friend was going to die.

"You need to go," Blam said. "Get out of here!"

Donovan reached down one more time into a pocket and produced a tube of black camo paint. He popped it open and began spreading the black paste all over Blam's face and hands.

"Stay low in these bushes and do not move." He pushed some leaves and fallen limbs over Blam's body, covering him in the camouflage of the jungle.

Removing the RIO's pistol from his holster, Donovan placed the handgrip in Blam's palm. The RIO gripped it as tightly as he could, but the gun slipped to the ground.

Donovan tried again, but this time he placed Blam's hand in his lap and his finger against the trigger.

"I'll be back with the cavalry. I promise," said Donovan. "You just hold on, okay, just—" The lieutenant tried to choke back emotion, but his voice cracked.

Reaching out for him, Blam placed a strong hand on Donovan's forearm. "You're the best friend a guy could have, Verner," he said. "Watch your back, pal. Now go!"

Donovan rose and hesitated. He looked at Blam and smiled as his eyes began to water. He feared this would be the last time he ever saw his best friend again. Donovan nodded and with that, he was gone.

Donovan cut through the jungle at a full sprint. He tried not to make any noise as he traveled the overgrown jungle at top speed. There were no roads, no trails, and no landmarks to indicate he was moving in the right direction. Several times Donovan stopped and checked his compass against his map. He needed to make sure he was heading toward the pick-up point. It was a good thing he'd paid attention in land navigation class, or he'd be in a world of hurt right about now. He didn't even have the stars to guide him, thanks to the canopy of trees shielding the skies.

Donovan couldn't believe what he had done to Blam, and it was eating at him. One of the codes of being a soldier is "leave no man behind." Still, he knew that neither of them would have made it out of that situation alive if he had stayed.

Their only chance for survival was if Donovan got to the evac point in time. Then he could call in Blam's position for pick up. That way, Blam might just make it.

Might, Donovan thought. *Who am I kidding?*

He stopped running for a moment, trying to catch his breath. For more than forty minutes, he'd been at full sprint, putting as much distance between himself and the crash site as possible. Through fear and exhaustion, doubt started creeping into his mind. The emotions building up inside of him exploded in a burst of his hot tears.

What had he done? He'd left his best friend, scared and all alone. And for what? To save his own hide?

Donovan thought of Blam sitting against that tree, bleeding, left to suffer in the jungle. He'd surely die of blood loss or at the hands of the enemy.

There's no way he'll hang on until the morning, Donovan told himself. *I should have stayed! I should have fought!* The lieutenant slammed his fist against his thigh with anger.

Feeling dizzy, Donovan reached out toward a tree for balance, but he missed completely. Stumbling, Donovan felt the ground below him give way. A complex structure of tree limbs and hemp rope snapped and fell apart beneath him. They had been camouflaged by leaves and twigs.

Luckily, Donovan shifted his weight. He moved just in time as a man-sized pit open up beneath him. Crawling to its edge, he looked down and cringed. A hole about ten feet deep, five feet across had been revealed. At the bottom of the hole, thick bamboo poles faced upward, their tips sharpened into deadly points. Each pole had been smeared with dried animal feces to promote infection. This was a punji stick trap.

Donovan had heard Marines on the carrier talk about these booby traps. He never believed they were actually real. Punji sticks were used by the Vietcong in preparation for an ambush, with the enemy soldiers lying in wait to pop out and surprise the Marines. The plan was that U.S. soldiers would dive for cover and impale themselves on the poisoned bamboo spears.

The sight of the trap made Donovan's stomach turn. *How could anyone do such a horrible thing to another human being?* he wondered. Then the lieutenant looked at the gun in his own hand. Was one weapon more horrible than the other?

A sharp noise caught Donovan's attention. In a flash, he spun, raised his weapon in the air, and took aim. Eyes wide, the lieutenant hesitated to pull the trigger.

A Vietnamese girl, about six years old, and her fifteen-year-old brother stood frozen in front of him. Fear washed over them. They didn't dare move.

"You American?" the boy asked in broken English.

Donovan raised his empty hand in the air. He lowered his pistol and nodded.

"We saw plane crash," the boy said. "That you?"

Donovan nodded again as he measured up the boy. He was about five feet, four inches tall and dressed in a blue shirt with black cotton pants. Both of the children's feet were clothed in leather slippers, which appeared to be made from scraps of water buffalo hide.

"Come with us!" the boy said. He turned and pointed behind him. "Village not far. Patrols many here. We hide you!"

Lieutenant Donovan was wary of the goodwill. He wasn't getting much of that these days, and he wasn't sure why these kids would want to help him.

The little girl walked over and placed a small hand on his forearm. She smiled. "We help," she squeaked.

Donovan stood, holstering his weapon, and grabbed the girl's hand. She and her brother led him deeper into the jungle.

***

A short time later, Donovan walked into what looked like the world that time forgot. Small grass huts, called hooches, made of bamboo frames and mud-covered turf, lined the dirt road. Some of the huts had small wooden fences surrounding the sides or backs of the homes. Livestock, such as pigs and chickens, roamed throughout most of the tiny village.

Though morning was just about to crack over the horizon, Donovan could tell the village was still asleep. Only a few open windows flickered with candlelight. High above, banana trees rose a hundred feet into the air, allowing protection from the tropical sun and plentiful harvest come picking time.

Donovan thought there was something peaceful about it all, like the way a Midwest farm must have been at the turn of the century. The land was untamed. The Vietnamese people were hoping to conquer it and better their society and culture. Donovan respected those goals. He hoped to craft his own plot of land when he finally returned home.

The children led Donovan across the dirt road and into their home. The lieutenant ducked through the curtain-covered doorway. The home was modest and small. Pieces of matting covered the dirt floors. Furniture was sparse, not even a couch. A simple set of handmade wooden chairs surrounded a small table, which had been crafted out of pieces of bamboo.

Donovan didn't have a second to rest. The children's mother came charging out of her bedroom as soon as the lieutenant entered. She took one look at the U.S. soldier and began yelling at the children.

The mother pointed at Donovan and screamed in Vietnamese at the young boy. He waved his hands in the air, pleading with her and trying to calm her down.

"He needs our help!" he said in his native language, but his mother didn't seem to care.

"No," she replied. "No! He does not stay here! You make him go! All he'll bring is death to this family!"

"If we don't help him," the boy replied, "then we're no better than the soldiers that burn our homes!"

Donovan slumped down on the bench, exhausted. Even as the mother screamed, he took a moment to relax and let the rest of the world fade away.

Donovan looked at his watch and frowned. The face had cracked somewhere along the line. But the antique watch was keeping perfect time. The second hand ticked from one hash mark to the next. *Great,* he thought, *I can't even keep grandpa's watch safe, let alone myself.*

Donovan did a double-take. Precious time was slipping away. Had it really already been two hours? Was Blam still alive? Would they be able to get to him even if the U.S. soldiers picked him up on time? Donovan's thoughts turned to fear again. Fear for Blam. Fear for himself.

Donovan wondered if this was how his uncle Michael felt during World War II. He had been trapped behind enemy lines in a small farmhouse in Germany on D-Day in 1944. Though his uncle didn't talk about the Great War much, he had taken Verner aside shortly before leaving for Vietnam.

His uncle looked young Donovan dead in the eyes, and said, "Fear is only an emotion, Verner. If you can control your fear, you can make it through anything. It took me a while to figure that out in France. You, however, should never forget it."

Now, Verner Donovan understood those words better than ever, especially as he studied the family that'd taken him in.

The boy was afraid of sitting by and doing nothing. If he didn't help the Americans fight this war, then he'd be no better than their enemy. The mother was obviously afraid of getting caught with an American fugitive. She knew the Vietcong would punish her swiftly.

And the little girl? Donovan looked over at her again. She stood in the corner of the small room staring at him. He tried to smile at her, but she was suddenly afraid of him. Obviously, what her mother was saying to them in Vietnamese was beginning to sink in. The black camo paint streaking his face probably didn't help either.

Donovan reached in his pocket. He pulled out a chocolate bar in a brown and silver wrapper. As he began to peel the aluminum foil back to reveal the soft, sweet bar underneath, the young girl's eyes went wide.

Donovan reached out and offered it to her. Slowly, she walked across the room and took it from him. The adult-sized candy bar dwarfed her little hands.

The chocolate had started to melt in the heat of the humid jungle. With every bite, candy smeared across the girl's face and cheeks. The child plopped down next to Donovan, no longer afraid.

He pulled out his compass and map to double-check his coordinates. Donovan saw the clearing for pick-up was only about half a mile north from his current location. He decided to get moving. "Look, kids, I appreciate what you did and are trying to do," the lieutenant said, folding his map. "But I gotta be somewhere in—"

The sound of an engine outside suddenly caught everyone's attention. Even the hysterical mother became suddenly silent. Lunging at him, the mother grabbed Donovan by the back of the collar and shoved him into her room. Then she shielded the entryway with a curtain as two Vietcong soldiers stormed into the home, armed with AK-47s.

As the men glanced around the room, the mother quickly gathered up her children. She pushed them behind her for safety. On the other side of the curtain, Donovan quietly crouched. He removed his pistol from his holster and cocked back the hammer.

The taller Vietcong soldier pushed past the mother and looked around the room. He explained to her that they were looking for American soldiers involved in a plane crash about four miles away. "Have you seen them?" he shouted. "They came this way."

The mother shook her head as the shorter soldier flipped over the table.

"Tell us!" he demanded.

"No one is here," she yelled back as the soldiers began tearing apart the room, looking for the American.

The short soldier glanced down at the little girl. The chocolate smeared across her face made him start to laugh. "Ha! They're so poor, they're eating mud now!" he exclaimed.

The tall soldier turned to see for himself. Crouching, he held the little girl's face. With a finger he swiped at the mud and smelled it. Looking down, he saw the candy bar still clutched in the girl's small hand.

The soldier rose and glared at the mother. Without warning, the man lashed out. He struck the mother on the face. "Where are they?!" he shouted.

The mother buckled to the floor, clutching her head. The little girl ran to the corner of the room, collapsed, and began to cry. Knowing he needed to do something to protect his family, the teenager rushed the soldiers, but a boot to the chest sent the boy reeling to the dirt floor.

Then the shorter soldier racked the heavy metal action on his weapon. He chambered a round and raised his rifle in the air, about to open fire on the mother.

Suddenly, the wall to the hooch exploded open as Donovan burst in from the other room. The lieutenant tackled the short soldier to the ground. The other Vietcong soldier turned to open fire, but the trigger jammed. His weapon was on safe.

This brief moment was all the time Donovan needed. He spun and got off two quick shots. The tall soldier fell over the legs of the table and rolled onto the dirt. He wouldn't be getting up.

The short soldier lashed out. He hit Donovan in the face with the butt of his rifle, causing the lieutenant to roll off of his Vietcong enemy. Kneeling, the soldier spun his weapon around and took aim at Donovan. As the soldier was about to fire, the young man leaped to his feet, jumping in between Donovan and the soldier.

A single shot discharged from the enemy's weapon. On the far side of the room, the teenage boy collapsed to the ground. Blood gushed from his chest.

Donovan turned to fire, but his aim was off. He missed the soldier, but the shot was enough to scare the man off. The Vietcong hastily exited the hooch and drove off in his truck.

Meanwhile, the mother rushed to her son's side. She cradled him in her arms as precious life seeped from his chest.

Donovan tried to apply some life-saving techniques. The mother wouldn't let Donovan near him. She just held the lifeless body of her son close to her. She yelled at him in Vietnamese and pointed to the door hysterically.

"Go!" the mother screamed.

Donovan looked over at the little girl. She was unharmed, but terrified. She sat huddled under the broken table, crying.

"I...I'm sorry," pleaded Donovan. "I..." But there were no words he could say. There was nothing he could do to fix these wounds.

The lieutenant picked up his gun and ran into the morning light, but he couldn't escape his problems. All around him, the lieutenant heard shouts and loud bangs. The sounds came again, but this time, they had many, many friends. Finally, he figured it out. He was hearing the shouts of Vietcong soldiers coming up behind him, firing in his direction.

Breaking from the cover of the bushes, Donovan ran into an open field. He scanned the skies, radio to his ear. "The LZ is hot! I repeat, the LZ is hot!" he yelled as bullets whizzed by. "Where the heck are you guys?!"

Above him, the whumping of large metal blades chopped through the air. A Marine UH-1 helicopter ripped over the trees and hovered on his position.

"Keep your pants on, Iron Hand One Three Niner!" echoed over his radio. Donovan looked up and saw the chopper crew chief throw a rescue hoist out of the bird.

As it hit the ground, Donovan climbed into the harness and gave a thumbs-up to the chief.

Like a worm on a hook, Donovan rose through the air attached to the cable. On the ground, coming out of cover of the trees, Vietcong soldiers opened fire on the chopper. The helicopter dipped and swayed, trying to evade the bullets.

Several rounds ricocheted off its hull and pierced the canopy. One round pierced the bottom window, shattering the lower cockpit. The pilot ducked. "Come on, Marine, get some!" he shouted to the gunner.

In the doorway, the sergeant manning the M-60 machine gun ratcheted the charging handle. He squeezed the trigger. The weapon sprang to life. Brass casings flew out of the ejection port and rained to the ground below. The enemy soldiers scattered and ran, diving for cover.

Still dangling from the cable, Donovan shielded himself from the enemy fire. Scalding-hot shell casings rained down on him in buckets. Looking up, he could see how far he had to go. But from this height, going down was an even worse option.

And that's when Donovan saw him. The short soldier, who had killed the young teen, was breaking cover of the trees. He kneeled on a dirt road and stuffed a rocket-propelled grenade into a shoulder-mounted firing tube.

Donovan tried yelling a warning to the gunner, but he wasn't close enough to the doorway. The sergeant couldn't hear him. The sounds of the battle were too loud.

As Donovan hung in the air, slowly rising toward the chopper, he skinned his .45 pistol. The lieutenant took aim at the Vietcong soldier below. The man had lifted the heavy RPG onto his right shoulder and flipped up the aiming site.

Donovan brought the gun up, sweat rolling down his face, and aimed. While lining up the sights, the words of his Marine marksmanship instructor echoed in his head. "Just point and squeeze!" they repeated.

Then Donovan squeezed the trigger. A single brass casing flipped end over end out of the weapon. On the ground, the short soldier's shoulder jerked to the right. He tripped backward, pulling the trigger on the RPG as he fell.

Donovan's eyes went wide. The grenade flew right at them, a trail of bright white smoke flooding the air. Thankfully, the deadly explosive careened right, missing the chopper and flying by the front of the aircraft.

Finally, after what seemed like an eternity, a sergeant grabbed Donovan by the scruff of the neck and yanked the lieutenant into the cabin. "We've got him!" he shouted to the pilot. "Go, go, go!"

The gunner finished his job. Then he stowed the weapon and slammed the cabin door shut. The chopper banked left, picking up speed. Streaking away over the thick jungles of Vietnam, Donovan watched through the door window. The rising sun cast an eerie orange-blue hue over the tropical wilderness. This would be a sunrise he would never forget.

***

A few weeks later, Verner "Candy Man" Donovan sat on the edge of a hospital ward bed. White cotton sheets felt alien to him now. Running his hands over the smooth linen, he couldn't help but think of that Vietnamese mother having to clean up the mess he'd made.

Her dirt floors covered with rattan matting. The rattan matting now covered with her son's blood.

"How are you, Donovan?" said a voice. Entering through the main hatch was the ship's skipper, Captain Harold Neef.

Donovan stood. "Ready to fight, sir," he said.

The captain smiled. "Why don't you take some downtime, son," he said. "Fall out of rotation for a while."

"No, sir," Donovan interrupted. "With all due respect, I'd like to be on the detail that goes in for Blam, sir."

Steely-eyed, he looked Donovan in the face. "Blam's dead, son," the captain said.

"The Vietcong, did they—?" Donovan started.

The captain slowly shook his head.

"No, the enemy never found him," said the captain. "You hid him well, son. Corpsman with the unit thinks he just fell asleep from the blood loss and didn't wake up, if that's any consolation."

Donovan nodded. "It's something, sir."

The lieutenant looked up at the captain. "He was my RIO, my friend. I —" Donovan stopped. He choked back tears. His gaze wavered as his eyes shifted to the floor. "I was responsible for him. I failed him."

"You didn't fail anyone, Donovan," the captain said. "Look at me, son. You did everything you could. Blam knew it would mean both your lives if you tried to save him. There was no way he would let you do that. Understand me?"

Donovan nodded again. "Sir?" he asked. "Is it all worth it? What we do?"

Quietly, the captain turned and sat down next to him on the bed. He thought about Donovan's question. Finally, he sucked in a breath and looked up at the lieutenant.

"There's a bigger picture out there, son," the captain responded. "Bigger than you, me, and even bigger than this ship. It's that bigger picture that matters because when liberty is taken away from somebody by force, it can only be restored by force."

Donovan nodded.

The captain continued. "But when it's given up voluntarily, that's when it can never be recovered," he said. "Pilots, and even RIOs, volunteer for this duty. We know the risk. We face that risk every day knowing our sacrifices make a difference in the bigger picture."

Donovan was touched by the captain's words, but it didn't stop the hurt of knowing his best friend's life was over. The captain rose and headed toward the main hatch of the carrier.

"Blam's still gone, sir," Donovan said quietly.

The captain stopped in the hatchway and smiled. "Son," he said without pause, "as long as you remember the man, he'll never truly be gone."

Donovan saluted his skip. "Aye aye, sir," he said.

CAPTAIN
ANNE DONOVAN

ORGANIZATION:
U.S. Army Nurse Corps
CONFLICT: VIETNAM WAR
LOCATION: AP BIA MOUNTAIN, VIETNAM
MISSION: Captain Anne Donovan heads to the front lines. Along with a small medical unit, she'll provide aid to the soldiers at Hamburger Hill.

EMERGENCY OPS

The overhead PA system blared: "All personnel, hear this! Incoming wounded on the pad!" The voice echoed through the camp, signaling the start of another long day.

The hospital staff sprinted down the lines of tents with medical gear clutched in their hands. Captain Anne Donovan, running up alongside one of the nurses, grinned. "What do you hear from the corpsman underground, Kathy?" she asked.

Together, the women hoofed it over the dusty road toward the sound of the approaching wounded. RN Kathy Martin furrowed her brow with sadness. "Looks like a squad of Marines were ambushed on patrol," she answered.

Donovan frowned. "You know the drill," she said. "Concentrate on the ones we can save—stabilize them and rush them to pre-op."

"And the others?" Nurse Martin asked quietly.

"The others..." Donovan's voice trailed off as the two women spotted the metal chopper skids hit the ground.

In an instant, the medical teams swarmed the helos and began unloading the wounded.

Even for a nurse like Captain Donovan, this was a grisly and frightful sight. She had only been in Vietnam for three months. Though she put on a brave face for the other doctors and nurses, seeing these wounded men—these boys—hurt her to her core. She hoped it would never stop being frightening.

The helos had delivered fifteen soldiers, all with life-threatening injuries. Medics strapped them to stretchers. Then they lined up the wounded in order of those they knew they could save. Those who didn't have much time left got sent to the back of the line.

The soldiers had been ambushed, unaware of what was happening until it was too late. Their injuries showed it. U.S. Army Rangers were regarded as the strongest of all the fighting men, but in this war, the Vietcong had home-field advantage.

Many of the Rangers onboard the choppers had AK-47 bullet holes and shrapnel wounds. Others had been unlucky enough to fall into homemade traps. These were holes dug into the ground by the enemy, and then covered with a camouflage netting of trees and twigs that disguised pits of deadly bamboo poles. One Ranger had taken a death trap through the chest. He'd lost a lot of blood, but he wasn't the worst casualty. Many of the boys weren't going to live through the day.

Donovan looked at Martin, whose eyes were welling with tears. "Make them comfortable," she ordered.

Then, kneeling next to one of the wounded U.S. Marines, Captain Donovan smiled. The young man grimaced back at her in pain, his morphine wearing thin. "Are you an angel?" the Marine asked softly with a Southern drawl.

Donovan shook her head. "No, I'm a nurse."

"Oh, thank the Lord," the man replied. "I was afraid you were here to take me away. How's it look?"

Donovan opened the Marine's blood-soaked shirt.

"You're lucky," said Donovan.

And he was. A grenade had exploded next to the soldier. However, the explosive had landed in thick mud, which had safely dispersed the explosion.

"Pre-op! Now!" Donovan shouted. "I want this Marine prepped and on the table in five minutes."

Nurse Martin immediately crouched down and opened her field kit. She placed an IV in the soldier's arm and taped the needle down.

Donovan ordered the nurses to haul the injured man out of the area. The nurses lifted the stretcher and rushed him toward the surgical tents as quickly as they could.

Running alongside the stretcher, Captain Donovan checked the Marine's vitals. She held his bottle of plasma high above her head. "Don't worry, Sergeant Ford—" she started.

The young man stretched out a bloody hand. He wrapped it around Donovan's arm. "Bobby," he said quietly as the two Army corporals carried him with care down the path.

Captain Donovan looked at the man and grinned. There was something there, an instant spark between them. "Bobby," she repeated. "We'll get you back on your feet in no time, sir."

"I hope not," Sergeant Ford replied. He let out a pained laugh. "You're the best thing I've seen since I landed in this Godforsaken jungle."

"You're a charmer," said Captain Donovan. Then she took off in a sprint, barking orders as medics neared the operating room tent.

***

Twelve hours. Most nurses at Hotel Meatball could count on spending that much time in surgery each and every day. But when Captain Anne Donovan, her white scrubs stained with the blood of several men, exited the surgical tent, time wasn't on her mind. No, she was focused on something deeper and more painful. She needed to keep the emotions inside, keep them bottled up. If she let them slip out, Donovan knew she'd never seal them up again.

Donovan tried to shake it off, that feeling of dread that was becoming worse with every hour spent in the operating room. Experiencing death was part of her job, but this was different. The things she'd seen in these last few months would stay with her for life. Donovan knew that, but she also knew she was a soldier now, not just a nurse. And those boys needed both.

Never in her life had Donovan imagined this much death. The sight was becoming more than she could bear.

The soldiers' wounds weren't accidental mishaps. These were violent injuries. Worse of all, they were intentional.

Stop thinking like that! Just stop! Donovan told herself as she slowly made her way out of the operating tent. She headed toward the far end of the army camp.

The sun was gone, and stars littered the night sky. Captain Donovan walked behind a tent. She removed her cap and threw it on the ground. Slumping down onto a wooden crate, she pulled a pack of cigarettes from the pocket of her uniform.

Donovan searched her pockets for her antique lighter, but she couldn't find it. "Oh no, where's Grandpa's lighter?" she said. "If I lost it, I'll—!"

Just then, cast in the glow of the full moon, a long shadow passed over her. "This what you're looking for?" a voice said. "Those things will kill ya, you know."

Donovan spotted Dr. Brian Woods, an Army colonel, lifetime soldier, and the Chief Medical Officer at the camp. Woods held a brass World War I trench lighter in his hand.

"So will the hours," Donovan joked. She took the lighter, lit her cigarette, and placed it back in her pocket.

A small metal thermos in one hand, Woods moved slowly toward the boxes.

"Find your own crate. This one's taken." Donovan smiled and crumpled the package of smokes in her hand.

"This was my spot before you got here, ma'am. You're trespassing," Woods said, dropping onto the makeshift seat.

"Guess rank does have its privileges, eh, colonel?" Donovan replied.

"And what kind of nurse smokes, anyway?" Woods asked.

"The tired kind," Donovan answered.

Donovan and Woods took a minute before either said anything. They just sat there, eyes skyward, gazing at the stars.

"How'd your team do today?" Dr. Woods finally asked, unscrewing the lid from his thermos.

"Eighty percent, sir," Captain Donovan said softly.

"Better than me," replied Woods. He sipped at the warm coffee he'd stolen from the mess tent. "I had bullet wounds of all kinds—AK-47s, M1911s, you name it. Heck, one even entered the soldier's leg and bounced up into his stomach."

"We had one kid, barely twenty," Donovan began. "A pilot. He'd been—" the captain stopped short. Her voice began to crack, and she lowered her gaze.

After a moment, the captain took a deep breath and then continued. "He'd been shot down by a MiG-21," she said. "Ejected safely, but the kid had already been cut up pretty bad by shrapnel. He was bleeding everywhere."

Woods whistled with concern.

"The doc put him back together," Donovan said, "and spent the next four hours pulling pieces of sharpened metal the size of dimes out of his chest cavity."

"But he's going to live, right?" asked Dr. Woods.

Captain Donovan nodded.

"Then you did your job," Woods said.

"That's not good enough, sir," Donovan said. She stood, throwing the pack of cigarettes on the ground. "It's like every kid they bring in here, we patch up with spare parts so he'll be good enough to put back on the line. We're not saving lives, we're just delaying the inevitable."

"You see yourself as a healer, is that it?" Woods asked.

Donovan nodded. "Yes, sir."

"Then what are you doing in my army?" Woods asked, glaring up at her.

"I thought I could come here, help Americans—"

"Bull," Woods interrupted. "You could've worked at a VA hospital to do that. Why'd you really come here?"

Captain Donovan waited a moment. Then she looked down at her commanding officer. He took another slow sip from his thermos.

"To prove something—" Donovan began.

"To who?" Woods shot back. "What, Daddy didn't get a son, is that it? You went off to go to war to prove you were worthy of his love?"

"No, sir, Daddy got his son, and he's an F-4 pilot," Donovan replied. "No, I wanted to prove it to myself."

"Prove what?" Dr. Woods prodded.

"Prove I actually had what it takes to do this job," said the captain. "I thought if I could come out here, be on the frontier of medicine, on the edge…I could prove I could someday be a doctor." All at once, the tears came streaming down her face. Wrapping her arms around herself, Captain Donovan stood in the moonlight, sobbing.

Finally, after a moment, Woods rose. His stern, angular face had softened. He placed a hand on Donovan's shoulder and smiled. "Heckuva place to do a residency, huh?" Woods said. Chuckling, the doctor wiped Donovan's tears away from her cheeks.

"Yes, sir," Donovan answered quietly.

"The fact you're having this kind of reaction to what's going on around here tells me you're going to be a terrific doctor," said Woods. "One of the best I've ever seen, Donovan. But you're no soldier."

Slowly, she looked up at him. "What?"

"We're not healers here, we're mechanics," said Woods. "It's our job to keep the machinery running, day in and day out. Slap spare parts on them and get them back into the fight. You look at these kids as people with families…"

Woods shook his head and paused for a moment.

"You can't," he said. "Bedside manners have no place in a combat zone. We get these boys back onto the line so they can fight the good fight. We're assemblymen fixing a war machine—and they're the cogs."

"That's horrible!" Donovan exclaimed.

"I know," Dr. Woods said. "But that's the way it is. After you get them walking, then show some compassion. Until then? It's your skills as a nurse they need, not your compassion. Can you do that, Captain?"

Donovan nodded. "How do you do it, day in, day out around here?" she asked.

"I'm a soldier, and a doctor," Woods said. "It's my job." He picked up his thermos, screwed the top back on, and turned to go. "Tomorrow, I'm pulling you from duty, Captain. I want you to take some time out of the operating room."

"But Colonel—" started Donovan.

"No buts, Captain," said Woods sternly. "For the next two weeks, I want you to do your rounds, and then when you feel up to it, I want you to go on the MEDCAP. Understood?"

"Yes, sir," said Captain Donovan.

"Fine. Now—" Woods waved at the pack of cigarettes on the ground. "Put those in the trash," he said. "I won't accept littering in my post."

With that, Colonel Woods walked back into the operating tent, leaving Donovan with her last cigarette and her thoughts.

***

The post-operation tent was a tomb, filled with eighteen men resting after surgery. All of the post-op beds were in two lines. There were ten beds on each side, creating an aisle between them. At the foot of each patient's bed was a small metal clipboard hanging from a metal loop. These were medical charts that listed each patient's vital statistics for the supervising nurses to review each hour.

Captain Donovan walked down the aisle surveying her patients. She looked over when she heard a familiar voice from behind her.

"Hey, Angel!" the man said.

Smiling broadly, she ducked her head so the speaker couldn't see her expression. She composed herself, and then turned around.

"Sergeant Ford," she said, walking over to the foot of his bed. She took his chart and examined it.

"Bobby, remember?" he said, a sly grin on his face.

"Yes, I remember," she answered. "Your vitals look pretty good, Bobby."

"Thanks to you, Angel," said the soldier.

"Well, you just get better so we can get you outta here, okay?" Donovan said.

Ford's grin vanished. "Wait, I'm not going home, am I?" he said anxiously.

Walking over to his bedside, Captain Donovan sat down in a small wooden chair. She leaned over to him, placing her hand on his wrist and checking his pulse. "Nope, you're going to be just fine in about two weeks. Back in the saddle with your unit," Donovan said as she timed his heartbeats with her watch.

"You scared me," said Ford. "I couldn't imagine leaving my boys behind. Most of them are too young to shave, let alone be Rangers." Ford paused for a moment. "I need to help 'em along, you know?"

Donovan smiled at this. She had felt the same way about some of the men that had passed through her care.

"Back in the saddle, eh?" Ford said. "Where you from anyway?"

Clutching the clipboard to her chest, Captain Donovan looked up and brushed the hair away from her eyes. "My family's originally from Illinois, but I grew up in Cheyenne, Wyoming," she said.

"I knew it!" exclaimed Ford. "I'm from Laramie, Texas. I knew I heard a twang in your voice." He tried to sit up, but stopped at the first sign of pain in his chest.

Donovan placed a consoling hand on his shoulder. "The twang only comes out when I'm angry," she said. "So easy there, Ranger, or you'll get to hear more of it."

"I hope so." Ford smiled as he lay back down.

Donovan walked over and replaced his chart at the foot of his bed. "You get some rest," said the captain. "And be more careful next time, will ya?"

"Not a chance," he said, struggling into a sitting position despite the obvious pain. "It's the only way I'll get to see you again, Angel."

Shaking her head, Captain Donovan turned to go. Then she narrowed her eyes, turned back to him, and smiled. "Look me up after the war, G.I.," she said softly. "You know where I live."

Ford beamed. "Count on it, Angel," he said.

***

The weeks ran on, and Captain Donovan was starting feel more at ease with herself and her assignment. Though she'd never admit it, the colonel had been right to take her off the surgery rotation and put her on post-op watch. Helping with the recovery of the men, not facing every hour of the day with another trauma, allowed her to focus and take note of what she'd need to do to survive.

The MEDCAPs didn't hurt her situation either.

Since the United States was technically in Vietnam to stop the spread of communism and oppression and help the local people, the U.S. Army periodically sent doctors and nurses out on Medical Civil Action Program operations. The MEDCAP doctors and nurses delivered much needed medical supplies, vaccines, and assistance to the local people of Vietnam.

Captain Donovan and Nurse Martin were scheduled on MEDCAP missions in the area near Phan Rang. With fellow doctors and nurses, they'd dispense medicines to the locals and set up public health programs. This included treating the sick and providing entire villages with anti-malaria medication, topical creams, and other antibiotics.

Tucked inside a village chief's hut, Donovan and Martin received a long line of children, varying in age and gender. Donovan sat at a small table, marking off information on several charts and lists as Martin gave shots to the children.

"Come on, dear," Martin said as one of the little girls refused to sit down, a frown pursed upon her lips. Every time

Martin came close to her with the hypodermic needle, the little girl backed away. Frustrated, Martin slammed the syringe on the table.

"What's the matter, Martin?" asked Donovan.

"She won't let me give her the shot," Martin said angrily.

Captain Donovan crouched down next to the little girl and smiled at her. "You don't want the shot?" she asked.

The little girl shook her head and frowned.

"But you want to feel better, don't you?" Donovan asked.

The little girl nodded. Captain Donovan casually reached over and picked up the syringe. "Listen, if you don't get the shot, you're not going to be able to grow up big and strong, okay?" she told the little girl. "And you want that, right?"

The girl hesitated, and then nodded.

"Then show me what a big girl you are, okay?" Donovan said. She rolled up the little girl's sleeve and took hold of the child's arm.

Eyes closed tight, the little girl waited in anticipation. To Donovan's surprise, the girl didn't even flinch when Donovan pushed the needle in.

"Not so bad, huh?" Donovan said as she wiped the girl's arm with an alcohol swab. "Sometimes, the things we don't know scare us more than the things we do."

Standing on her tiptoes, the little girl kissed Donovan on the cheek and then bounced off and out of the hut.

"Let's take a break, okay?" Donovan said.

"You're really good with them, ma'am. The kids, I mean," Martin said. She and Donovan strode along a path. They passed by the small huts that made up the main part of the village.

Captain Donovan shrugged. Then she looked over at the small, dark-haired heads throughout the village. "They just deserve a chance to be kids, you know?" Donovan said.

Martin looked at the silver captain's bars on Donovan's collar. "That's why you became a nurse," she said.

Nodding, Donovan looked at Martin. She cocked her head to the side. "That, and the long hours," she said. "Nothing like staying up all night on a school night."

"Why'd you join the Army, ma'am?" Nurse Martin asked.

"College, mostly," Donovan said. "Do a stint in the Army Reserve, and they pay for me to go to medical school. Who knew a war would break out?"

Donovan let out a nervous laugh. "And how about you?"

"I wanted to see the world, get out of Podunk, Indiana. Make something of myself," Martin said as she looked around her. "I didn't know I was going to be in a M.A.S.H unit, though. I thought I'd be in the green zone, helping the wounded there, you know?"

"We've been pretty lucky," Donovan said. "According to the colonel, some of the hospitals have been coming under fire, snipers trying to pick off the chopper pilots and doctors on the pads." Donovan looked into the jungle. "I wouldn't be surprised if we're in someone's crosshairs right now."

"Don't say that!" Nurse Martin said, angrily waving her finger at Donovan.

Smiling, Donovan shrugged. "Sorry about that," she said. "Bad joke."

"All due respect," replied Martin. "I don't understand how you can be such a softy on the inside but outwardly...callous."

A look of shock spread over Donovan's face as she stopped and stared at Martin. "Is that what you think of me?" Donovan asked. "That I'm just hard?"

Frowning, Martin shook her head. "Well, no," she said. "But you do make some off-handed comments sometimes. To hide the fact you're scared, just like the rest of us."

"I see," Donovan said softly.

She'd never thought of herself in that way, so this came as a huge surprise. Even during her residency at Laramie County Hospital, Donovan had always been the one who treated people with respect and equality.

"Like the time Nurse Rose wasn't sure about the dosage of aspirin to give a soldier," Martin said. "And you told her to throw some in his mouth, and whatever landed in there was the right dosage."

Donovan chuckled. "Yeah, I can see how she might have misconstrued that," she said, grinning.

"Or the time—" Nurse Martin began.

"Okay, okay!" Donovan said, raising her hands. "I get it! I'll try not to take it out on other people, okay?"

"Yes, ma'am," Martin answered.

"Let's get back," Donovan said. "It's going to get dark soon, and the last thing I want to be is out here at night without a full MP escort."

***

It was several more hours before the medical teams made it back from the MEDCAP. Expecting evening chow, they drove the Jeeps into the camp but instead of a line at the mess tent, what Donovan and the others saw made their blood run cold.

The sun was setting, turning the sky an amazing shade of orange, but it was a backdrop to the chaos in the camp. A frenzy of medical personnel rushed from one tent to another. They fetched supplies as quickly as their feet could carry them. All of the personnel tents were empty, and the lights in the surgical tent, which at this time were usually dark, shone through the front flap.

Jumping out of the truck, Donovan grabbed her bag and rushed toward the O.R. Nurse Martin was close on her heels.

Nurses were shouting to corpsmen and other soldiers as they made their way through the crowds. "What's happening?!" Martin yelled

"I don't know," a nurse replied.

All at once, Donovan spotted a young man and grabbed his arm, stopping him in mid-stride. "Corporal Vetter, what the heck's going on?" she asked.

Vetter was panting hard, trying to catch his breath. "Army's trying to take Hill 937 again," he finally blurted out.

Donovan rolled her eyes and swore under her breath.

"Hamburger Hill?" Martin asked.

Donovan nodded sternly. "It's been five days! When are they going to give it up? There isn't any strategic value to—"

"All the wounded are coming straight here," Vetter said breathlessly, "and it's a total mess! And we're running out of everything—gauze, swabs—heck, even the plasma's running low. And now we're down one surgeon."

"What are you talking about?" Donovan asked.

"The aid station," Vetter said. "They set up an aid station near the front so they could patch up the light casualties and get 'em back on the line ASAP, but their doc was killed. They need a new doc there pronto."

"We're short-handed," Donovan said, shaking her head. "Who's Woods sending?"

"Himself, ma'am," Vetter said. "Major Woods is going out there personally."

"With who?" Donovan asked.

***

After tossing his medical bag into the back seat of a Jeep, Colonel Woods ran over and pushed open the motor pool door. He looked up to find Donovan staring him in the face.

"I'll ride shotgun," she said.

"Absolutely not!" Woods shouted. "This is the deepest mess

these soldiers have been in, and I can't have anyone breaking down on me out there. This is the frontline in the bloodiest skirmish to date. There's a chance I won't make it back!"

"Sir, you know the book better than anyone," Donovan said. "You can't go all John Wayne out there by yourself."

Woods raised a hand, waving her off. "Screw the book! Those boys are getting slaughtered, and they need help now."

"And so do you," Donovan said. "You can't go without a nurse to assist you, and you said it yourself. I'm the best one you've got. Let me help you."

The more they argued, the more likely it was that men were dying. But Woods knew she was right. He could use a second set of hands.

"Fine," Woods finally said.

They loaded into the Jeep and he started the engine.

"But if I see one tear, you're outta there," Woods said.

"Then don't get all childish on me," Donovan said, "and control your emotions, sir."

Grinning at her, Woods slammed the shifter into first gear and rocketed out of the motor pool.

In the heat of the mountains of South Vietnam, in the western A Shau Valley, one peak rose high above the jungles— Ap Bia Mountain. The mountainside overshadowed the valley, towering at more than three thousand feet.

Ridge upon ridge reached up from the thick forests toward the peak. Trails wound up the sides through the dense bamboo groves and tall elephant grass. In some places, the vegetation was so high that even the soldiers riding in personnel carriers could not see above the pale, silky grass.

Ap Bia was known to the locals as "the mountain of the crouching beast". The Army called it Hill 937. Soldiers nicknamed it Hamburger Hill.

Night had fallen before Woods and Donovan arrived, and already the sky was lit up like the Fourth of July. Rockets soared through the air, muzzle flashes lit hot spots in the trees, and flares glided down on parachutes like falling stars.

For the past six days, hundreds of soldiers from the U.S. Infantry had been swarming this hill like angry ants, doing everything in their power to capture its hulking mass from the clutches of the North Vietnamese. But they had failed and continued to fail hard.

The 7th and 8th Battalions of the enemy's 29th PAVN Regiment had successfully kept the Americans at bay. Still, the U.S. Air Force had been pummeling the mountaintop for days, deploying thousands of pounds of ordnance, including the deadly chemical napalm.

With thirty-five Americans dead and at least one hundred wounded, something had to change to ensure their success. But tactics came from a different part of the Army than what Captain Anne Donovan and Colonel Woods were familiar with. None of that mattered to them as they stood in a small tent a mere kilometer from the majority of the fighting. Here, with limited support from the combat medics, they spent the next eleven hours on their feet, operating on the wounded.

One after another the soldiers came, with injuries ranging from missing limbs to massive skull wounds and everything in between. Only some of the wounded could be saved. For the rest, Donovan and Woods tried to make their passing as comfortable as possible. It wasn't easy.

The smell of cordite wafted through the air from nearby explosions. The doctors had to yell at one another over concussive blasts that shook the ground around them.

Though the treatment space was smaller than their own operating room, each doctor navigated the clutter well. Still, only the most rudimentary tools were at their disposal. The innards of a medic's kit sprawled over a small table. Scalpels and forceps swam in an alcohol and blood mixture on a small metal tray. A battery-powered ventilator chugged on the floor beneath them, and a small suction machine hissed in the darkness.

It was crude and gruesome, but somehow they still managed to save lives.

The floor was littered with filth. Cleanliness wasn't their major concern here. Used sponges and bloody gauze sat crumpled on the wooded planks. In the back, a small post-op was set up with a team of medics doing the finishing work. The surgeons needed to concentrate on the more difficult and life-threatening procedures.

On either side of a small surgical table in the center of the room, Woods and Donovan worked diligently. They were doing their best to save the young man in front of them.

Blood ran from a small hole in his leg, and though they had sewn the femoral artery back together, the wound was still pumping red, sticky liquid onto the floor.

"I need suction!" Woods yelled.

Just as Donovan turned on the suction device, a mortar blew up next to the tent. Dirt and debris flew in through the tent flaps. Donovan leaped onto the soldier's body, protecting the open wound from contamination.

"One more like that, and we might as well give it up," Woods said.

With a pair of forceps, he dug deeper into the man's leg. "Got it," he exclaimed, slowly removing the lead slug from the man's thigh. "Time to close him up!"

A pair of soldiers came over, took the patient off the table, and carried him to another part of the tent. There, his wound would be stitched back together.

"Next!" Donovan yelled. She pulled her surgical mask away from her face. Then she looked over at Colonel Woods, shaking her head.

"How many's that?" she asked tiredly.

"I lost count at fifteen," Woods admitted.

Suddenly, two soldiers came running in, an unconscious G.I. carried between them.

Blood coated his uniform and his helmet was slung low, shrouding his blackened face from view.

"What've we got, Corporal?" asked Donovan.

"He's been shot up pretty bad," one of the soldiers said. "And the flyboys dropped a load of napalm. Looks like he was caught on the edge of it. We just found him on the hill. He's barely breathing." The soldiers angled the wounded man toward the empty table.

Donovan cleared the last patient's debris and made hasty work cleaning the area. "Get him on the table," she said as the corporals did their best to set him down softly.

"Get his helmet off," Woods ordered.

The medics reached over and unclasped the chinstrap. The steel pot fell away from the dying man's head, finally revealing his face for the first time.

"Okay, let's—" Donovan stopped as she looked down. She had recognized the injured soldier.

"Hey, Angel," Sergeant Ford whispered. His jaw had been broken in several places from multiple bullet impacts to the face.

Donovan went into shock. Her muscles seized. She was unable to move. Her crystal blue eyes searched for a glimpse of what was once his proud, strong face.

"I —" she tried to speak, but words wouldn't come.

Ford tried to smile, but his cheek muscles didn't work. He was dying and everyone—especially Donovan—knew it.

Colonel Woods slipped an entire syringe of morphine into Ford's arm, allowing the warm fluid to ease the sergeant's pain. It was the only thing he could do for him. All Donovan could do was to hold Sergeant Ford's hand in hers.

Ford tried his best to speak. "Don't—" he forced out. It was so soft that Donovan needed to lean down, her ear to his mouth, to make out the rest of his words.

"Don't…cry…Angel…" he whispered. "Least I got to… see you again. I'll be waiting for you. But…don't meet me too quickly…okay?"

Donovan placed her gloved hand against his charred face, cradling it in her palm. "Okay, Bobby," she said softly, fighting hard to keep back her tears, to be strong for him.

For a moment, the sounds of the war—the explosions, the screams, the gunfire—seemed to disappear. Donovan watched Bobby Ford close his eyes and slip silently away, his body going soft and limp, his head slumping into her waiting hand.

And then, he was gone.

Woods slowly placed a white sheet over the sergeant's body and motioned to the corporals to take him away.

"Do you want to go back?" Woods said quietly, turning to Donovan. But she raised her hand and placed her surgical mask back over her face.

Taking a deep breath, Donovan turned to the doorway. She looked out. "Next!" she yelled.

***

Twelve days had passed since the battle of Hill 937.

By day ten of the assault, eighteen hundred men from five infantry battalions of the 101st Airborne—along with ten batteries of heavy artillery, 270 sorties flown by the Air Force, more than 450 tons of ordnance and more than 60 tons of napalm—led the U.S. troops to finally capture the hill.

Though the mission was a success, the mainstream media reported it differently: more than three hundred American soldiers were wounded, and seventy-two were killed in action. Civilians at home pondered the relevance of this action, and the cost of the massive mountain in the middle of the jungle was weighed against the value of American lives.

The mountain lost.

Americans were already unhappy with the U.S. presence in Vietnam. But now, things grew steadily worse. The anger and confusion of people back home began to trickle down to those serving in the war. Many soldiers in-country became unmotivated to fight. Even commanding officers were finding it hard to blindly follow orders from Washington.

But back at Camp Meatball, nothing changed. They still treated the injured and patched men up as best they could— only now Captain Anne Donovan finally understood her role in Vietnam. The motor pool had been made into a staging area for the long, cold metal boxes that contained the remains of fallen soldiers. Here, they waited until they could be laid to rest on American soil.

And here, among the rows of the dead, Anne Donovan found the coffin of Sergeant Bobby Ford.

Donovan placed a soft hand on the top of the box. Her body shuddered at the feeling of the cool aluminum casket.

"Such a cold place for such a vibrant man," she whispered.

"Donovan?" a voice called from the door.

Turning, Donovan saw Colonel Woods enter the room, his cover clutched in his hands. "I read the letter you wrote to Ford's mother. It was beautiful," he said.

She turned from the coffin and faced her commanding officer. "I wanted to thank you, sir," she said.

"For what, Captain?" Ford said.

"For teaching me why it's important to be a bit distant in what we do," Donovan said. "Teaching me how to be strong. Not just for myself, but mostly—" Her gaze drifted over the metal boxes sitting motionless in the darkness. "—so I can be strong for them."

Colonel Woods nodded. He looked around the massive holding area at the hundreds of boxes waiting to be shipped back to the States.

"Well," he said, "as long as we're passing out thank yous, guess I owe you one as well."

"Me? What for, sir?" Donovan asked.

"For reminding me that even though I'm a major, I'm a human being first. And not the other way around."

Donovan nodded at her commanding officer.

The blaring sound of the P.A. system burst out into the darkness: "Attention! Attention! All personnel, incoming wounded on the pads!"

Looking back at Woods, Donovan smiled. "After you, Doctor."

Shaking his head, Colonel Woods waved his hand at the door. "Ladies first, Captain."

Donovan looked him square in the eye. "I'm no lady," she said. "I'm a soldier. Come on."

She led him out into the night, alive with the hum of helicopters.

LIEUTENANT COMMANDER
LESTER DONOVAN

ORGANIZATION:
U.S. Navy SEALs

CONFLICT: WAR IN AFGHANISTAN

LOCATION: KANDAHAR, AFGHANISTAN

MISSION: When a SEAL team Seahawk helicopter goes down in the icy mountains of Kandahar, Lieutenant Commander Lester Donovan must make a difficult decision—follow orders or go "off mission" and save his fellow soldiers.

CONTROL UNDER FIRE

The temperature of the wind that blew over the SEAL's face amazed him. Most times, one welcomes a breeze on a summer day, but not here. Not in this place.

Afghanistan was an entirely different beast. It was hot, like a blow-dryer. The granules of sand that swirled in the breeze made the wind even more unwelcome. The SEAL squinted, doing his best not to get sand in his eyes. But even though sand kept pounding at his face through the open door of the flying SH-60 Seahawk, he was a happy man.

Today saw mission accomplishment for Lieutenant Commander Lester Donovan, Team Leader of 2nd Platoon, SEAL Team Two. It was an especially sweet victory because it was Donovan's first outing as their commanding officer. The Team had always respected Donovan's leadership, but a couple of older sailors had initially questioned his promotion.

To them, Donovan seemed like a by-the-book officer. He wouldn't bend on situations the master chiefs knew they might encounter down range. They wanted a commanding officer who could adapt and be as flexible as the situation demanded.

Donovan understood this type of sidestepping. He didn't like that some sailors felt they were above the law. He knocked the Team back pretty hard sometimes, but they respected him for it. He was also, hands down, the best shot in Team Two. He could pick fleas off a dog from 100 yards with just the iron sights of his gun. And he knew this impressed the men, especially the older guys, even if they never showed it.

This mission was about as textbook as a SEAL operation could get, and it had gone off without a hitch. A standard snatch and grab. They had been tasked with the capture of Taliban leader Majad Raman Hassan, and they had gotten him without one casualty. The sixteen men of 2nd Platoon were all coming home alive and well. Eight of the SEALs rode in the first bird. The second eight occupied another Seahawk helicopter not far off their starboard side.

Seaman Second Class Williams, the team's sniper, chuckled as he looked out the helicopter door. He closed his eyes and let the wind whip his face. "This is just like back home!" the big southerner said as he basked in the heat.

One of the other SEALs, Petty Officer Kaili, the team's corpsman, just snarled. "Of course you love this, you BBQ-eating, Texas-Longhorn hillbilly. Man, all you Southern dudes just dig the heat! Me?" Kaili made a wave-like motion with his hand. "I'm a water man, myself."

"That's 'cause you was born on an island in the Pacific, brah," Williams laughed and hula danced with his hands. "Where's your grass skirt, Hawaiian boy?"

"At your mom's house, *haole!*" Kaili laughed.

The old man of 3rd Platoon, Master Chief Petty Officer Miller, just smirked and shook his head.

"There he goes, droppin' the mom bomb again," Miller said. "When are you gonna come up with something new?"

"As soon as you can start keeping up!" Kaili shot back.

"Ohhhh!" the men all shouted and laughed.

Donovan was proud to be a part of this team. They were a tight-knit band of brothers. They made fun of each other, tossed around macho jokes, and played all day long. But they trusted each other with their lives. Behaving like a family strengthened that brotherly bond, but when it came time to do their jobs, playtime was over. They became locked on like laser sights and were the best at what they did.

Team Two were known in the Special Ops community for being experts at cold weather warfare. They trained for months in Anchorage, Alaska. They were snow masters. They could go anywhere it was cold and beat the enemy at their own game. Team Two was ready for the winters in Afghanistan.

In a post-9/11 world, U.S. President George W. Bush decided the best defense against terrorism was a strong offense. He ordered troops into Afghanistan to attack the Taliban where they slept.

That decision meant fighting in caves deep in the snow-covered mountains of Kandahar.

As seasons changed, the SEALs of Team Two traded in their parkas for moisture-wicking tactical t-shirts and went hunting for a second tour. Hunting in the super-hot temperatures and sand-swirling winds.

After a devastating ambush weeks earlier, many members of the Team had made the ultimate sacrifice and new leadership was sought.

Enter Donovan.

Having proven himself an invaluable Team member, Donovan was given an unwanted battlefield promotion. His Team Leader had been killed in action entering a warehouse to evict local terrorists who were hiding there. Only through fast actions and motivating leadership did Donovan help his SEALs bring a relatively positive close to an otherwise messy situation. Back at headquarters, he found himself promoted to the lead position—though he never wanted it. Especially not because his Team Leader had died.

The Seahawk helicopters dipped, floated across the sands, and passed over farmhouses. The prisoner in Donovan's chopper looked out the main hatch as the farming village slid by underneath them. He frowned as he looked at the ground and started mumbling.

Kaili bent forward and whispered in the terrorist's ear. "Pray all you want. Ain't gonna help you, brah," he said.

The man turned and glared at Kaili for a moment. Then he continued praying quietly.

Looking starboard, Donovan saw the other half of his team riding in the other Seahawk. He grinned as he placed a hand up to his ear and yelled into his microphone. "Alpha Three, Team Leader, over?" he said.

In the other chopper, a young lieutenant, Mike Barnett from Huntsville, Alabama, looked across the gulf of hot air at his commanding officer. He smiled. "What can I do for you, sir?" Barnett asked.

"How's everyone doing, over?" replied Donovan.

"Riding high on the—" Barnett began.

There was a flash of sparkling light and a brilliant blast of heat. Donovan watched in horror as the nearby chopper instantly became a burning mass of twisted metal.

A glance at the ground told the story. A team of three men stood on a berm on the far end of one of the farms. They were reloading rocket-propelled grenade launchers with fresh ammo. The Seahawk had been shot out of the skies by a Taliban RPG team.

Reacting quickly, Donovan turned to the cockpit, yelling into his microphone. "RPG! RP—" he shouted.

He was cut off in mid sentence as the tail rotor of his aircraft exploded and detached. It splintered into a million metal shavings that littered the skies. The chopper spun. It twisted in the opposite direction of the rotors as it fell.

The ground rushed up quickly. The pilot did his best to rotate and slow the chopper's descent, but it didn't seem to help. In a matter of seconds, the chopper slammed into the sand and burst into flames.

Inside, the men were shaken and rattled. The explosion had cracked through the cabin, killing four of the sailors and knocking the master chief unconscious.

The pilot had done his best to save his passengers and crew. But the chopper's control panel had caved into him and his co-pilot, killing them both.

Donovan had been knocked against the main cabin bulkhead during the crash. He was dizzy and immobile. He saw nothing but the white haze of smoke, the orange glow of flames, and his men dying.

A concussion was the least of his problems. He was vaguely aware of five robed men, obviously locals, reaching into the inferno. They pulled his high-valued target from the rubble.

Majad Raman Hassan had been liberated.

A low, steady hum and a high-pitched ringing filled Donovan's ears. Unable to focus, the lieutenant commander tried to reach for his weapon, but he couldn't find it. It had come out of his holster and been tossed across the wreckage.

The Taliban took everything that wasn't nailed down. Equipment bags, weapons, ammo, explosives. And worst of all, they took the survivors.

Majad Raman Hassan was now free to give orders again.

The terrorist pointed at Williams and Kaili, both still alive. The men were dazed, but they tried their best to fight back. For their efforts, the aggressors beat them senseless.

Donovan tried to move, struggled to help, but there was nothing he could do. His safety harness wouldn't budge. Blackness rapidly washed over him like oil seeping into the water. And all of a sudden, his world was dark.

***

Licking at his hands, the cabin flames woke Donovan from unconsciousness. As he looked around, dazed, he'd almost forgotten his situation. Then the sight of the charred remains of his teammates lying across the wreckage snapped him back to reality.

A slight moaning, coming from under the layers of warped sheet metal, made him turn. "Master Chief!" he yelled, reaching for the pieces of steel pinning Miller to the ground.

Donovan dealt with his pain as he pried away the hot sheet metal, but it was slow going. Outside, the fire moved dangerously close to the fuel flowing from the tanks. The flames grew hotter. Donovan knew they only had a few moments before the entire chopper went up like a Roman candle.

Struggling, Donovan could feel the metal budge. Miller looked up at his chief officer. They both knew there wasn't any more time.

"GO! Get the heck outta here, sir!" Miller grumbled as Donovan strained to lift the heavy metal.

The flames inched closer to the fuel stream.

"Sir, please! Leave me, just—just go!" cried Miller.

The metal began to move. Donovan was able to jam his shoulder under the plate. Now he could use his legs for leverage.

As the metal shifted, Miller scooted from under the heavy materials. The flame finally touched the leaking fuel. Once the fuel ignited, a burning stream of fire started barreling toward the chopper at an uncontrollably fast rate.

Donovan quickly helped Miller to his feet. As they stumbled from the helicopter, Donovan grabbed the only remaining piece of equipment that hadn't been stolen or destroyed—a canvas weapons bag. The SEALs bolted from the crash as the fire finally reached the fuel tanks.

The enormous eruption created a shock wave that rippled through the air and slammed into both men. They tumbled and rolled to the ground as flaming debris sailed past them.

They lay on their backs, breathing heavily. Looking at Donovan, Miller smiled. "Glad you did all those boot camp exercises now, sir?" he said with a laugh.

Donovan grabbed at his back. "I know you are! Who knew all those squats would save your life?" he replied.

Miller grinned as he opened the canvas bag. He pulled an M4 carbine out of the container and snapped a suppressor on it. "It's Williams's gear bag," said Miller. "We've got two M4s with silencers, two MK23s, and a butt-load of ammo for both.

Some other goodies in here, too, but I'd say it's just what we need to rescue our—"

Donovan cut him off. "No."

The thirty-seven-year-old master chief turned to the younger lieutenant commander. Donovan began loading his M4 with a fresh magazine of ammo.

"What do you mean, 'No'?" Miller asked, shocked.

"Exactly that," answered Donovan. "Our first priority is to get outta here and report what happened."

"No way, sir!" Miller stood, ratcheting the charging handle of the weapon. "We need to jump out there and get our boys back from—"

"From who?" Donovan yelled. "When you were face down in the wreckage, did you see who took them? Where they took them? Or even which way they went?"

"No, but—"

"But what, Master Chief?" Donovan asked. "We don't even have a starting point. No communications, limited supplies, and no idea of where we are."

He took the second M4 from the bag and loaded it. After slinging the bag over his shoulder, Donovan stuck the butt of his rifle into the sand and held it still. Since he knew their location on the globe and the time of day, Donovan could get a compass bearing based on the way the shadow of his weapon fell on the sand.

Donovan looked at his watch.

Sadness fell over the lieutenant commander. Cracked and splintered, the glass lens of the watch's face was barely holding on. The old Bernus WWII watch was an heirloom. It had been passed down from generation to generation of military men in his family. When he signed up for Officer Candidate School, Donovan's father had given it to him. This had been his great uncle's watch. He'd worn it during his jump into Normandy in WWII. When he came home, he'd given it to his brother, Lester's grandfather, before Korea. It had then passed from Lester's grandfather to his dad when Verner was shipped off to Vietnam.

The watch meant a lot to the family. Lester often heard stories of its travels across the globe. But when his father had given it to him, Lester had been floored. His father had told him, "If you're going to be part of the service, then by God, you're going in as a Donovan!"

Service hadn't been his father's wish for Lester. He'd wanted Lester to follow his dreams, to become a journalist, to report on the world, not to be a part of its bloodshed. Their family had given enough to the country.

But after the attacks of September 11, Lester Donovan knew he couldn't stand by and let other people take risks protecting his personal freedoms while he reported on it. He wanted to be part of something bigger than himself. He wanted to be on the front lines of a war that needed people like him—natural leaders.

His father and grandfather were proud of Lester when he got his golden "Budweiser" Trident of the Navy SEALs at graduation. After the helicopter attack, and the loss of their Taliban prisoner, Lester wondered if they would be proud of him now.

But the watch kept ticking, even though it had been smashed, and that made Donovan smile. If the watch could keep working, he could, too. The falling shadow from the weapon, plus the time from his watch, soon gave him a compass heading. "We go that way," he said, pointing. "The Hindu Kush mountains."

Miller's eyes narrowed. It was going to be a rough hump, but they could do it. Water was all they needed, and hopefully they could find it along their route.

Miller looked over to Donovan. "I know what the book says, sir," he said, "but I really think we need to find our men."

"This was planned," said Donovan. "They knew our route, and they shot us out of the skies. I know you think I'm new and I don't care, but you're wrong. If I knew where they were, if I had any clue, we'd go in there back-to-back like Rambo and Marcinko. But I don't, and neither do you. Their tracks were cleared away by the wind, and all I know is that the base is north from here." Donovan adjusted his bag. "We've got a long hump, so let's get moving. I'll take the lead."

With those words, the conversation was over. They were heading back to base and that was final.

Donovan could tell that Miller wasn't happy, but he believed there wasn't any other option.

Somehow, the Taliban figured out the path of the choppers, and that was important information. They were one of three Teams sent out to capture targets in the area. This couldn't happen to the other ones. Miller and Donovan had to get this info back to base soon.

The sun was sinking on the horizon, and Donovan knew it would cool off quickly. Even a nightfall of 85 degrees was better than high noon in the desert. Sand kicked away from their Special Forces' boots as they slowly, cautiously trekked toward the mountains.

***

Within hours, their plans had changed. The mountain ridge was shorter than they'd expected. Miller and Donovan explored the area and soon came upon a hideout. Most strongholds of this type were usually just holes in the side of a mountain that looked like they were made by gophers. But not this one. This one was well hidden by large outcroppings of rock and natural stone formations that surrounded the mouth of the stronghold.

It's like the entrance to the Batcave, Donovan thought. *No wonder we missed this one.*

The ridgeline didn't allow them as much cover as he would have liked. But it didn't matter to Donovan who lay in the dirt, looking into the mouth of the cave about two hundred yards ahead. They were going to have to go in the front door either way. This was just another challenge.

To the left, a small generator sat, chugging away and belching black clouds of smoke into the air.

The lines from the old generator ran into the mouth of the cave, obviously feeding the area with electricity. To the SEALs, it was a yellow brick road, leading to the place where the Taliban were probably keeping their soldiers.

The two Americans quietly used their hands to move the sand and dirt from underneath them. They dug in for the long haul. They needed to observe the area, making sure they learned all they could about the men inside. If that meant sitting still and watching, no matter how long it took, then that's what they would do.

Donovan rummaged in the equipment bag. A smile crossed his face as he pulled out a foot-long, remote-controlled airplane body.

Miller smirked. "That's gonna make life a whole lot easier."

The RQ-11A Raven UAV was ready for flight. After switching on the remote, Donovan had the infrared camera send data to the handheld video device. He clicked on the silent motor and threw the small plane into the air. The drone flew off without a sound and swept into the night.

Both men took shifts flying the drone and reviewing the data it was transmitting back. Several hours passed before either of them had anything to report.

Soon, however, they located the same five robed men from the attack. Out front, two guards on a roving patrol were relieved every two hours. Of the men that had made the switch, only one had repeated, so it was safe to assume they were correct in their counting.

The Taliban men were armed with rifles, but that seemed to be all. No explosives. No grenades. Their lack of weaponry would make things easier on the two SEALs.

"Okay," Donovan began as the Raven came back and landed next to them. "Here's the plan."

Donovan was to sneak toward the main entrance while Miller waited, perched in an over-watch position with his weapon, covering his movements. When Donovan was close enough to the front entrance, he would take out the left guard at the main entrance nearest to the generator. Then the master chief would snipe the other from his position.

At that point, Miller would join Donovan. They would cut the power to the generator, causing a blackout inside the cave. Hopefully, the Taliban fighters would assume that the generator was malfunctioning for some reason, forcing one of the other guards to the entrance. Then he would be hit, leaving only two to watch their prisoners inside.

Donovan was sure that they would find the place where the SEALs were being held. With reasonable losses to the enemy, they'd get their friends out easily, thanks to their night-vision goggles.

Miller laughed. "Reasonable?" he asked.

"I don't want a bloodbath," answered Donovan. "But if someone gets in your way, put 'em down because we're going home. With everyone."

"Including Hassan?" asked Miller, pulling a high-powered scope from his equipment bag. He locked it onto the top of his M4 carbine.

Donovan nodded. "If he's in there, he's going back."

"Hooyah, sir," Miller responded.

Donovan reached down and grabbed a handful of dirt. He spat on it, and rubbed it on his face. He looked over to Miller. "How do I look?" he asked.

Miller shook his head and smiled. "Like you should be eatin' worms."

Miller crawled to the left. Donovan made his way around to the generator and the cave entrance.

Crawling to the left flank of the generator took Donovan twenty minutes. When he finally got there, the changing of the guards was taking place.

Donovan waited patiently and quietly. The replacement guard pulled out a canteen of water and offered it to the other man. *Oh man, great,* Donovan thought. *I'm going to be here all night!*

But to his surprise, the man didn't want the water. The first guard left, leaving the relief to drink by himself.

Five minutes later, Donovan began to move.

He slowly reached down and removed the karambit knife from the sheath tied to his left boot. He held the knife in his hand so that its blade curved forward from the bottom of his fist. Then Donovan positioned himself on the balls of his feet.

He suddenly sprang forward. He covered his prey's mouth with his left hand. The guard fell behind the generator, and Donovan finished him.

As expected, when the first guard went down, the second guard on the right turned. Miller raised his weapon and fired. The enemy's chest jerked twice as shots entered his torso. He dropped to the deck. Miller's aim was spot-on.

Quickly, Miller joined Donovan at the mouth of the cave.

"Noise discipline," Donovan said. "Hand signals."

Donovan's night-vision goggles flipped down over his right eye and powered on. The blackness of night lit up in green and white hues.

With a thumbs up from Miller, they stepped inside. Weapons held high, their butt stocks pressed tightly to their shoulders, the men walked in step—Miller on the left, Donovan on the right. With every third step, they swept the weapons and made sure there was no one behind them.

The darkness glowed in hues of green as they explored the cave as silently as possible. Although they were taking it slow, their combat boots on the rocky and sandy echoed loudly.

A gradual slope of about fifty yards led downward into the mountain. The cave began to widen. Partially hand-carved, but mostly natural, the stone was smooth to the touch and damp. Donovan had always found this fact odd. He thought stone in the desert would be dry, but it seemed some of these caves were like sponges, sweating in the darkness.

The wires from the generator were their road map. Miller and Donovan followed them, fastened to the ceiling, deeper down into the darkness.

Suddenly, the beam from a flashlight and the sound of footsteps approached. Both men stopped. They flattened themselves against the wall in the darkness as a Taliban soldier came toward them.

One of the guards had been dispatched to see what was wrong with the generator. Unfortunately for him, Miller was waiting. Placing a hand over the enemy's mouth, the SEAL maneuvered a knife to the man's throat and pulled him in.

Donovan retrieved the fallen flashlight and shined it in the guard's face, blinding him. He questioned the man in Pashto. "Where are they keeping the Americans?" he asked softly.

Eyes closed tightly and his face full of fear, the man nodded and pointed. Miller removed his knife just long enough for the man to tell them the SEALs were down a passageway about 100 meters, then in the cavern to the right.

Donovan turned off the flashlight, and Miller finished the job. As the terrorist's body crumpled to the floor, the men moved on. The SEALs turned a corner and stopped in their tracks. This wasn't just a cave for five men. It was a massive subterranean network of caves that led into other parts of the countryside. There were dozens of passageways that branched off from here. Donovan and Miller had just traveled into the lion's den.

This was a junction point for all enemy operations in this part of the country. Three separate underground passageways led off in front of them to other parts of the desert. As far as they could see, those three passageways had several different branches that opened up farther down into their own system of maze-like tunnels. One tunnel on their left led into what looked like a small storage room. The one to the right was where they assumed their U.S. comrades were held.

Usually, these types of caves were just dead ends, with only enough room for a cot and a lantern. Not this one. This was more like a subway system for terrorists.

Donovan had heard rumors of this place but had never believed them. Seeing it, he was speechless.

"They...they must have been working on this for years," Miller whispered, breaking the silence.

Nodding, Donovan looked to the front-right passage, where two other men appeared with flashlights. The Taliban soldiers were heading right at them. If the SEALs didn't move, they'd surely be discovered.

Moving left, they ducked into the small storage room. Donovan and Miller flattened themselves against the walls as the two men passed by.

Donovan bumped something. He turned to see several wooden crates piled high against the walls. Tapping Miller on the shoulder, he thumbed at the boxes.

"A weapons cache," whispered Miller.

Several crates of AK-47s and RPGs sat ready to be used against other NATO soldiers. The weapons that had shot down their chopper had come from here. This fact was obvious because, more importantly, his team's stolen gear sat on a table behind the boxes.

Donovan picked up ammo, pistols, night-vision goggles, and even plastic explosives. He placed it all into a canvas bag and tossed it over to Miller. The master chief slung it across his back. "For the boys," Miller said.

Donovan nodded, looking around for more goodies.

"Yeah, and let's leave these guys with a bang. Sound good?" Miller asked.

Donovan agreed and motioned for Miller to wire up the crates with the explosives. Miller took a small brick of Composite Four out of the equipment bag. He began to mash it up and spread it along the edges of the crates like a thick line of toothpaste.

As he searched around for whatever else he could find, Donovan looked toward the end of the small room. He suddenly stopped and smiled.

On the end of the small table, sat an old-style Vietnam-era radio. He lifted the handset, turned a few of the frequency dials, and was about to hit TRANSMIT, when something caught his eye. A detailed topographical map lay on the table, marked up in red pen. Lines and shapes circled and connected U.S. troop locations and movements from all across the region. The enemy had done their homework. Through their own type of recon, the Taliban had learned deployment schedules and the U.S. timetables for patrols.

They've got everything on us, our entire mission. They must have been watching us for months, a year even! Donovan thought. Instinctively, the lieutenant commander grabbed the map, folded it up, and shoved it into his pocket.

Donovan cautiously pressed TRANSMIT and whispered into the handset. "Ghost Hunter Actual, this is Ghost Hunter Two, do you copy?" He released the transmit button.

Nothing. Just a low static. His heart sank. Maybe the battery was dying, maybe they were too far out of—

"Ghost Hunter Two, this is Actual, go ahead," suddenly crackled out of the handset.

A large smile crossed Donovan's face as he pulled a small, folded map from his right cargo pocket.

"Man, are we happy to hear you!" Donovan said. "Ghost Hunter One is gone. We are currently involved in CSAR operations and need emergency evac at these coordinates." He read off their location into the handset.

"Roger," said the radio operator. "We will have someone to you in thirty minutes."

"Also request a bunker buster air strike at this locale. We're sitting on a group of terrorists in underground tunnels. It's like Grand Central Station down here," Donovan said softly.

"Roger that," said the RO. "Air strike approved at those coordinates. I suggest you make haste."

"Like rabbits in mating season," Donovan said. "Out." He placed the handset on the table and moved over to Miller, who had just finished setting the explosive charges.

"Timer?" Miller asked.

"No—detonator. Here, you take it," said Donovan. "Might need it to cover our exit. We've got thirty minutes. If we can't do it in that time, we're all dead anyway."

"Okay," Miller replied. He pulled the magazine out of his weapon and slapped the back end of it against his leg. He made sure all the brass was packed neatly in the clip. After slapping it back in, he pulled back the charging handle and got ready to rock. "Let's do this."

Silently, they moved from the storeroom and crossed into the dark hall. Three Taliban with flashlights were standing there, complaining about the lack of power. One of them was on a radio, reporting to someone outside, who was trying to figure out where the guards were. Donovan listened to the conversation.

"I've got three tangos. Two men outside at the generator. Can't find the guard," Donovan translated for Miller.

"We've got five minutes max," Miller replied. "Say when."

The master chief raised his weapon and took aim. Donovan did the same.

"Take 'em!" Donovan shouted.

All the men heard were whooshes of air as the silenced shots flew from the barrels of their M4s. Like sacks of wet potatoes, the three terrorists hit the ground, their flashlights clacking on the hard stone floor.

***

In a nearby room, Williams and Kaili, badly beaten, knelt on the dirt floor of the darkened cave. Their hands were tied behind their backs by hemp ropes.

Behind them, two large guards, both holding hacksaws, stood quietly. They were ready to perform their sworn duty to execute the prisoners in the most horrific manner. A metal tripod topped by a small HD video camera waited to capture every frightful moment of the execution.

"Cursed lights!" the Taliban leader yelled. "You think we would have replaced that generator by now!"

From behind him, the fourth man in the room laughed. "Not to worry, Rojan," he said. "We will be rid of the infidels soon enough. It's probably just out of gas again."

Hassan entered, a piece of paper in his hands.

"It's nice to have you back, brother," the cameraman said as he slapped Hassan on the back. "How's the speech coming?"

On the ground, the two prisoners wheezed. Their raspy breathing echoed out into the small chamber. Both men were in bad shape, having been tortured and beaten for some time. Kaili, the Team's corpsman, looked over at Williams.

Blood flowed from his teammate's ear. Bruises under his eyes had turned deep purple. His face was blue, his breathing getting harder and harder to push out with each minute.

"You hangin' in, brotha?" Kaili whispered.

Williams grinned. "Sure. Probably just my allergies."

"Keep the faith, they'll come for us..." Kaili said quietly.

Suddenly, a boot came down on the back of his neck, pinning him to the ground.

"No talking!" said Hassan from behind as he lifted his foot off of Kaili's neck. Reaching down, he grabbed Kaili by the hair and pulled him close, whispering in his ear.

"You'll have plenty of time to talk where you're going, brah," the Taliban leader joked. He slammed Kaili's head into the stone floor.

Kaili turned and glared at Hassan with a look that could melt marble. If he could get free, he'd show that guy a thing or two.

"DOWN!" a voice echoed into the room from nowhere.

Without hesitation, Kaili, who knew that man's voice better than his own, dove left. He shoved Williams to the ground as strategically placed M4 rounds flew through the air.

The first to fall was the left guard. The 5.6-mm NATO round blew through his chest and exited into the wall behind him.

The second guard made a move for his AK-47, but two perfectly placed lead projectiles walked up his arm and into his pectoral muscle. They ricocheted inside his chest cavity and exited out the other side of his torso, killing him instantly.

Closest to Donovan, the cameraman struck out with a right hook, but Donovan blocked it with the barrel of his rifle. In one full sweep, he pushed the man's fist aside and rammed the silencer into his face, breaking the man's nose. Crumpling to the floor, the man was no longer a threat.

Majad Raman Hassan, on the other hand, was still alive. He spun on his heels and raised a pistol in the air. He aimed at the back of Donovan's head.

With the butt of his weapon swinging like a baseball bat, Miller cold-cocked Hassan in the skull. The leader lost the gun—and consciousness—as he fell to the ground.

Quickly, Donovan used his knife to cut his teammate's restraints. He looked at Williams, and could tell he was hurt badly. "I'm guessing he called them a lot of names they didn't quite like," Donovan said.

"More than you'll ever know," Kaili answered back.

"Can you walk?" Miller asked as he handed Williams and Kaili both MK23 pistols.

"I'll…I'll freakin' run out of here if I have to, boss," Williams wheezed back. He stood tall, but obviously in pain.

"Good, because we gotta go—!" Miller stopped short as the lights in the cavern flickered back on.

"And him?" Miller asked as he motioned to Hassan.

"All of us, Master Chief!" Donovan said.

With a disappointed sigh, Miller reached down, tied Hassan's hands together, and picked him up in a fireman's carry across his back. He balanced the unconscious man on his shoulders so Miller could still fire his weapon from the hip.

They moved out, Kaili taking point and Williams and Miller in the middle. Donovan checked the rear.

They made their way out of the holding area and into the hallway. All was clear for the moment, but as they rounded the corner into the central passageway, the men froze.

And that's when it happened.

Men flooded out of the passages like roaches in the light. The SEALs were immediately spotted and outnumbered. Shots from AKs rang out in the cave as fifteen Taliban terrorists took aim and did their best to stop the escapees.

Donovan took a knee as he returned fire. Bullets sprayed from his weapon. They chipped up all around them as they provided covering fire for one another. In typical SEAL style, they leapfrogged out of harm's way, as one after another, they peeled off the firing line. Moving to the rear, each man covered the other's movements.

The exit of the cave was about fifty yards away now as the terrorists continued their push. Miller threw off his night-vision goggles when daylight started breaking over the mountains and spilling into the mouth of the cave.

One of the terrorists stepped into the entrance. Hassan fell to the ground as Miller, fast as a cougar, pulled his knife out. In a quick glint of reflective light, the man at the foot of the cave was no longer a problem.

"Reloading!" Donovan yelled. He dropped the ammo magazine and reached for a fresh one. Kaili and Williams took careful aim with their pistols. The noise in the cave from all the automatic weapons fire was deafening.

"Move out!" Donovan ordered.

As Kaili and Williams ran, Miller aimed outbound, securing the exit ahead of them.

"Faster, faster, faster!" Miller yelled. Kaili and Williams finally came jogging up the fifty-yard slope.

Weapon ready, Donovan crouched at the junction of the central chamber and the main slope. To his left was the weapons storeroom. In front of him, more Taliban members came flooding into the open hall.

He fired a few covering bursts as he got ready to move, but two more Taliban terrorists ran out from behind the cover of the central passage and opened fire. Donovan dropped flat to the deck as hot lead slugs ricocheted all around him. He was pinned and couldn't move.

He tried to formulate a plan, but didn't have time to think. From the dark storeroom to his left, a single man launched into the air, a knife raised high, and lunged at him from the darkness.

"Ah!" the man shouted as he sliced across Donovan's torso, cutting the chest sling and causing his M4 to hit the ground.

Feet skidding on the sand that covered the entrance of the cave, Miller fired a three-round burst at a Taliban soldier coming up the main pathway.

Once outside, he could hear the distant sounds of rotor blades approaching from the north. Miller looked over at Kaili who was exiting. Williams was close behind, but Donovan was missing.

"Where's the commander?!" Miller yelled over the sounds of gunfire.

"He was right behind us!" Kaili answered as he looked back into the darkness of the cave.

"We've got about five minutes before this entire place goes up like Hiroshima!" Miller said, pointing to the sky.

He looked back into the abyss that he'd just fought his way out of, and then back at his teammates. Miller knew what he had to do. He dropped the magazine out of his M4 and reached into his vest for a fresh one.

Suddenly, over the top of the farthest ridgeline, Miller could make out the silhouette of the Seahawk chopper coming to rescue them.

"That's our ride! Get Hassan there!" Miller yelled as he reloaded his weapon.

"What about you?" Kaili asked.

"Don't wait! Go!" Miller yelled, running into the cave.

Inside, Donovan rocketed forward with a left hook. Though his fist flew wide and failed to make contact, the shattered fragments of glass on his watch caught the man. The glass sliced through the skin on his face.

The pain, cutting through his cheek and eye socket, made him scream out and drop his knife. Donovan dropped down, rolled, grabbed his weapon, and came up firing. One shot was all he needed. The bullet hit its mark.

Bullets continued to rain down on him as the other men approached from below. A sharp pain unexpectedly bit into his leg. He looked down and saw that one of the rebounds had pierced his thigh.

Donovan's leg gave out as he reached for the wound.

Ten more soldiers poured into the chamber as he dragged himself into the relative safety of the storeroom. He placed his weapon around the corner and pulled the trigger. Amazingly, three more Taliban soldiers went down. The others took cover.

Finally, Donovan's ammo ran dry, and he dropped his weapon. There was a moment of peaceful calm as all firing in the cave stopped. No one was sure what was going on. Had they done it? Had they killed him? Had they destroyed the American infidel?

One of the terrorists stood and looked around the corner of the center passageway, only to be met by a .45 caliber bullet from an MK23 pistol. He fell backward and the others again opened fire.

Knowing he only had four rounds left in his pistol, Donovan chose his shots carefully. Blood spilled from his leg. Then Donovan heard a familiar voice, yelling out behind him over the ruckus.

"Sir!" Miller yelled as he braved the onslaught of enemy.

Confused, Donovan looked back toward the front of the cave. Miller, M4 in the air, was laying down covering fire, trying to reach him.

Waving his hand in the air, Donovan shouted for him to get back. "Get outta here! Get to the chopper!" Donovan ordered.

Ten more men flooded into the main passageway. There were now seventeen Taliban soldiers advancing on them and the stone could only take so much abuse before their natural cover would be gone.

"I'm hit! I can't make it! Blow the C4 and go!" Donovan ordered as he fired off the last of his rounds.

Miller didn't obey. He managed to get to Donovan's position. Once there, he smiled and handed his commander a magazine ammo for his machine gun. "SEAL Team. We're here to get you out," Miller said with a grin.

Donovan said, "I told you to go!"

Reaching down, Miller took Donovan into a fireman's carry. Miller could move faster if his hands were free, but that would mean Donovan would have to provide covering fire.

"You said we all go home! Leave no man behind!" Miller shouted back.

They broke cover, launching into the hail of bullets that flew between them and the exit to the cave. An M4 in each fist, Donovan yelled bloody murder as he depressed the trigger on each weapon, firing fully automatic bursts at the enemy!

Several of the shots were true to their targets. Taliban terrorists dropped like marionettes with clipped strings and hit the deck in clumps of flesh. This was just enough cover for the men to get a head start on the enemy. Miller ran up the grade toward the exit fifty yards away.

Finally, with M4s dry and nothing to hold back the tidal wave of men, the enemy rose from their hiding spots and began to advance on the pair.

The SEALs inched closer to the mouth of the cave. Sunlight began to creep across Donovan's face. He looked forward hopefully, but the bullets that zipped past their heads reminded him they weren't home free yet. When he looked back, he saw the wall of Taliban soldiers bearing down on them.

As they made it to the mouth of the cave, Miller reached down and pulled the detonator from his pocket.

"Now, Miller!" Donovan screamed.

Miller closed his eyes and prayed as his thumb pressed the button.

The earth trembled. Detonators fired and ignited the C4 plastic explosive. In a huge flash, the front of the cave filled with smoke. Loose rock and debris fell on top of the Taliban pursuers.

The shockwave reverberated outward, smacking Miller in the back, making him lose his footing. Tumbling, he dropped Donovan to the deck and rolled onto the dirt.

Quickly, Miller rose and grabbed his chief officer. The sound of jet engines filled the skies above them. "Sir, we're not out of this yet!" Miller said. He picked up his wounded teammate and helped him to run.

Minutes later, as Miller and Donovan reached a safe distance, the Seahawk swooped in. Kaili helped the wounded commander into the bird as Miller pulled himself in.

"Thirty seconds to impact!" the crew chief yelled. The bird lifted off the ground as quickly as it had landed. Miller's feet were still dangling out the main hatch as it rose into the air.

A single bunker buster bomb fell from the skies, digging almost 75 feet into the ground before exploding. The hillside erupted in flames. Massive chunks of dirt and debris flew hundreds of feet into the air. The explosion shook the ground hard, the shock waves rushing through the underground maze. The entire terrorist hideout and its infrastructure were completely destroyed.

As the Seahawk helicopter flew across the desert toward base, a corpsman worked on patching up Donovan's leg. Luckily, the wound was a through and through, meaning it had gone straight through the muscle without damaging any vital systems. It would heal without permanent damage.

Donovan thought back to the crash in the helicopter.

His first thoughts after the crash had been for his men, not the mission. Would his grandfather have acted the same in Korea? His father in Vietnam? He was so worried about the safety of SEALs all over the world, he didn't even care that Hassan had escaped. Even when he was placed aboard the evac, he had asked about his teammates and demanded the corpsman deal with them first.

Williams and Kaili were going to make it through just fine. Seemed Williams had caught walking pneumonia and the specific blend of Taliban hospitality hadn't done much for it, but he'd pull through okay. And Kaili would bounce back quickly, his wounds being mostly superficial, but they'd keep him on light duty for about five weeks.

Though he was happy to hear it, Donovan was saddened by the thought of losing an entire fire-team of SEALs. His SEALs. Men he was personally responsible for. It felt devastating to him. The surviving members of his team were worse for the wear, but they were alive, and that was all that mattered in the long run.

Lying back against the chopper's bulkhead, Donovan sat, his eyes closed, feeling the vibrations of the bird moving beneath him. Under his breath, he mumbled, "I was supposed to be a poet...."

Miller frowned. "What was that, sir?" he asked.

"Nothing," Donovan replied. "Well, it's something Thomas Jefferson said: 'I was a soldier so that my son could be a farmer so that his son could be a poet.' My father said our family had given enough blood for our country and I didn't have anything to prove. But I told him there was too much injustice in the world and I was needed as a soldier, not as a poet."

A moment of silence passed as Donovan looked down at his leg and frowned. "Maybe I was wrong."

"Sir—" Miller began. He reached over and placed his hand into Donovan's cargo pocket. He retrieved the Afghani map he'd taken from the caves and handed it to his commander.

"I wouldn't be here and neither would any of these guys, if it weren't for your great leadership out there today, sir," Miller said.

Donovan raised an eyebrow at the master chief.

"And that yahoo," Miller went on, pointing over at Hassan, who was zip-tied and strapped into a jumper seat, still unconscious. "He would still be out there killing innocent civilians. So I'd say your father was dead wrong."

Donovan nodded. "Thanks," he said.

"Besides, sir, looks to me like you got both sides of the equation right," said Miller.

He nodded out the open door.

Leaning over, Donovan glanced out the hatch. The warm wind slapped sand at his face. Behind them, the remnants of the smoldering mountainside drifted high into the air.

"Me, I'd call that poetic justice," Miller quipped.

"Hooyah, Master Chief! Hooyah!" Donovan said.

LIEUTENANT COMMANDER
LESTER DONOVAN

ORGANIZATION:
U.S. Navy SEALs

CONFLICT: WAR IN IRAQ

LOCATION: BAGHDAD, IRAQ

MISSION: Lieutenant Commander Lester Donovan and the U.S. Navy SEALs must capture a known terrorist near the border of Syria.

HEART OF THE ENEMY

"This dustbowl is the armpit of humanity, if you ask me," a deep voice growled from the back seat of an armored Humvee. The vehicle cut quickly from one lane to the next. The driver did his best to swerve in and out of the traffic that blocked his path.

Traffic congestion in that part of Iraq was the stuff of legend. The men of 2nd Platoon, SEAL Team Two had become masters in the art of the "Slalom Slide," an unofficial driving maneuver that felt like a high-stakes video game. The team zigged and zagged around cars and pedestrians, bypassing the wretched bottleneck.

In the front seat, Lieutenant Commander Lester Donovan grimaced. He turned to face the man in the back seat. "What's your problem, Agent Upton?" the lieutenant asked.

Holding onto the headrest in front of him for support, Special Agent Bradley Upton, CIA, narrowed his eyes. He glared at Donovan. Upton's long face was boyish, hiding the fact he was pushing forty years old. "What do you think?" Agent Upton said angrily. "These people...all they do is blow themselves up. And for what? To make others conform to their way of thinking."

Petty Officer Kaili, the team's corpsman, had been sitting next to Upton for an hour, listening to him complain. "They've just installed democracy in this country," Kaili finally spoke up. "You gotta give it time, bro. Give them a chance to do something with it."

"Whatever," Upton grumbled. "They've been killing their own people for hundreds of years. Nothing we do is going to change that. Murdering innocent civilians to make a point isn't part of the democratic process. It's terrorism. And that's why I'm stuck out here in the hot desert sand and not back home in Washington."

The driver, Master Chief Petty Officer Miller, was the team's explosives expert. He was also the oldest member of the platoon. Taking his eyes off the road for a moment, Miller angrily glared at Upton.

"If it wasn't for CIA guys like you, funding all the secret wars back in the '80s," said Miller, "we probably wouldn't be here either, College Boy."

"All right, Master Chief, knock it off," Donovan said. He looked down at his handheld GPS tracking unit.

"Where we going anyway, sir?" Miller asked Donovan.

"To see the—" Donovan began.

Upton promptly cut him off. "You'll know when I decide to tell you, Master Chief," said the CIA agent. "Until then? I suggest you shut up and drive!"

Miller turned and whispered to Donovan. "This guy's really starting to get on my nerves, sir," he said.

"That makes two of us, Master Chief," Donovan replied.

"Okay, let's look alive," said Miller, as the Humvee rolled into a new part of the city.

To his left, Donovan could see a pair of legs sticking straight up from the Humvee's floorboards behind him. Donovan tugged on the man's camos. "How's it look topside, Williams?" asked the lieutenant commander.

Seaman Second Class Williams, the team's sniper, stood in the Humvee's turret. The upper half of his body stuck out of a small hole in the vehicle's roof.

Williams's Nomex-gloved hands were wrapped around the massive .50-caliber machine gun, which was anchored atop the Humvee. "Quiet as church on Sunday, sir," he yelled back down through the hole. Then he rotated the turret 180 degrees, scanning the area for signs of danger.

The truck swung left, kicking up dust from its tires. The two-lane road narrowed as the Humvee passed through a small alley. Then the road opened into an expansive courtyard, nearly the size of a football field. In this neighborhood, the typical tan and beige tones of desert buildings suddenly gave way to more lively colors like salmon and turquoise.

"Whoa!" Miller said. He whistled, impressed.

"Yeah, this is different," Kaili said, looking around at the unusually clean and lively streets.

Indeed it was. The streets and storefronts were free of trash, litter, and graffiti. The locals appeared to be orderly and polite. They waved at the soldiers and smiled as the Humvee cruised down the street.

"I don't care if people here are as nice as your momma back home," said Donovan. His eyes narrowed, scanning the area for the enemy. Usually when things got too quiet, he knew, trouble wasn't far behind. "Everyone stay frosty."

"Hey, Spook!" Master Chief Miller shouted at Agent Upton over the hum of the 6.6-liter diesel engine.

Glowering over at Miller, Upton sneered. He obviously didn't like the term "Spook" even though it was befitting his post. After all, he was a non-official government agent in the field, a cloak-and-dagger operative who made top-secret decisions from the shadows. Officially, he wasn't in Iraq. He was, in a sense, a ghost.

"How 'bout you tell us where we're headed?" said Miller. "What is this place? It's like the Twilight Zone."

"Fine," said Upton. "Police Chief Barana Hakedam, ex-warlord turned police magistrate, runs this area."

"Looks like he's done a bang-up job," Donovan said.

"Make no bones about it," replied Agent Upton. "He's an old Ba'athist supporter."

"Saddam Hussein's old ruling party?" asked Miller.

"The one and only," Upton said, signaling Williams to stop the Humvee. "Police Chief Hakedam patrols these streets with an iron fist. His brothers are his deputies, and he trusts no one else. Hakedam says blood is the only thing that matters."

"Seems like a nice guy," Kaili joked. "But why are we going to see him?"

Agent Upton hesitated for a moment. "He has information he's willing to trade for the whereabouts of Abdul Kasieem," he finally said.

"King Commerce Kasieem?" Miller asked, recognizing the name from military briefings.

"So you can read?" Upton said, laughing.

Miller held his breath, holding back his anger.

"I don't care who you are in the real world," said the Master Chief. "Talk to me like that again, and you'll go back to Washington, all right...in a box."

"Don't test me," the CIA agent shot back. "I can have you erased, if you know what I mean."

Miller cracked a small smile. He nodded back at Upton, letting their differences go for the time being.

"Then as you know, Abdul Kasieem is the number one black marketer in the entire Middle East," Upton continued. "If we get our hands on him—"

"We put a major dent in the weapons-smuggling business around here," Donovan finished.

"Finally," Miller said. "A mission that makes sense!"

On the corner of the next block stood a large, imposing Iraqi man. He was well over six feet tall, weighed two hundred pounds, and wore a dark green and khaki uniform.

It was Barana Hakedam.

Opening the front door, Donovan stepped out and opened his palms toward the air. "*As-Salamu Alaykum*," Donovan said, greeting the Iraqi police chief.

A smile swept across Hakedam's face. His pearly white teeth shone in the morning sun. "My friends! *Marhaban!*" Hakedam exclaimed. The police chief raised his arms in the air, welcoming Miller and Agent Upton as well.

Lieutenant Commander Donovan turned back toward the Humvee. "Williams, you and Kaili stand guard," he ordered the men. "Keep an eye on the vehicle. I don't want anyone taking off with our ride." Donovan slung his M4 rifle across his back.

"Yes, sir." Seaman Second Class Williams racked the action on the .50-caliber machine gun. He rotated in the turret, his eyes narrowed as he scanned the area.

"*Salam*, Police Chief Hakedam," Upton said, extending his hand warily.

Hakedam shook Upton's hand. Then he motioned toward the front door of his small police station. "Please," he said. "You must come inside and have some tea."

Following the Iraqi official, Donovan, Miller, and Upton slowly entered the building one by one.

Police Chief Hakedam and the three U.S. soldiers sat around a small wooden table inside the Iraqi police station. Hakedam poured steaming hot water from a teapot into a fragile cup. He handed it to Lieutenant Commander Lester Donovan and smiled.

"*Shukran*, Chief," said Donovan, taking the cup and blowing on the hot tea.

"I must tell you," Hakedam began. He poured a cup for Agent Upton and Master Chief Miller, and then one for himself. "You are the most respectful Americans we've had here. It is quite refreshing."

"You know why we're here, Chief," Donovan said politely. "What can you tell us about Abdul Kasieem?"

Reaching into his pocket, Hakedam produced a USB memory stick. He handed it to Donovan.

"Ah, yes," said Hakedam, setting his cup on the table. "Kasieem operates in the deep desert on the far side of Quasi, near the Syrian border."

Agent Upton snatched the USB device from Donovan. "Of course," he said. "That's a perfect location for smuggling items over the border."

"Kasieem sells to the highest bidder," said Hakedam. "The potential buyer makes no difference to him. Many have tried to find his weapons, to double-cross him, but none have ever returned. I have heard stories of sliced throats and screams echoing in the deep deserts. Not one man has ever been able to find the main fortress that contains his arsenal of evil. He and his men are ruthless killers who want nothing of Allah's ways. Kasieem is pitiless and cruel."

Hakedam took a cigar from his breast pocket and put it to his lips. Noticing, Donovan reached into his back pocket. He pulled out his small WWI-era trench lighter and flicked it on.

Upton studied Hakedam. He sat back, took a sip of his tea, and then looked at their host intensely. After a moment, he said, "Many have said the same of you and your brothers, Hakedam. That you are pitiless and cruel."

Before he could light his cigar, Hakedam threw it to the floor angrily. He slammed his fist onto the table. "You have insulted my family!" Hakedam shouted.

"No, you have insulted me," said Upton. "We already know everything you're telling us. We know you've had personal dealings with Kasieem in the past."

"The past, yes," proclaimed Hakedam. "I have changed since Americans came and overthrew Saddam Hussein." He slammed his fist onto the table again and again, shaking the cups from their saucers.

"Hakedam," began Donovan. The lieutenant commander reached out a hand, trying to calm the police chief. "Don't let the hasty words of this CIA spook get to you. We all know—us soldiers know—what you've built here, Hakedam. We know what you've done for the people of Iraq." Donovan glared at Agent Upton.

After a moment, Hakedam smiled. "Yes, yes, you are correct!" he exclaimed, and then he started to laugh. "Please forgive my temper, will you?"

Agent Upton didn't join in the laughter. "What's on this stick?" he asked, holding up the USB device.

Hakedam stopped laughing and looked at Upton, annoyed. "It is the location of his weapons cache and main compound here in Iraq," said the police chief.

Jackpot! Donovan thought. He shot a look over at Master Chief Miller. They both grinned.

"And what do we owe for the honor of this intelligence?" Agent Upton asked suspiciously.

"Nothing," said Hakedam. The police chief picked his cigar off the floor. He dusted it off, placed it in his mouth, and then leaned back in his chair with a smile.

Agent Upton glared at Hakedam. "Excuse me?" asked Upton. "You want nothing in return?"

"Consider it...a good faith gesture," said Hakedam. "You know, for future dealings. If I ever need something, I'll know I can count on Uncle Sal to help me out."

Donovan struck his trench lighter again and lit the police chief's cigar. "That's Uncle *Sam*," he explained.

"Same thing," said Hakedam. He rolled his eyes and jutted out his hand to Agent Upton.

After a short moment, Upton reached out and shook on it. "Done," he said.

***

The U.S. Forward Operating Base was located forty miles east of the Iraqi-Syrian border near the city of Tal Afar. Though Tal Afar had been plagued by terrorist attacks in the past, usually in the form of suicide bombings, the area remained a perfect staging area for the U.S. operation. The U.S. FOB was close to Kasieem's stronghold. Still, the base was far enough away that military presence wouldn't cause any suspicions to the local people.

"All right, let's go over it again," said Lieutenant Commander Donovan. He stood and pointed at a series of computer screens inside the intelligence tent.

Agent Upton stood, quietly listening, his arms crossed across his chest.

The contents of Hakedam's USB stick were splashed up on the screens. Huddled around the monitors, the three other U.S. Navy SEALs laid out their battle plan. On each of the three screens were satellite photo reconnaissance images of the coordinates given to them by Police Chief Hakedam. On the table, each of the men had a hard copy of the map.

"According to the intel provided by Hakedam and our low-orbit spy satellite," Donovan said, "Kasieem's stronghold is camouflaged as a small goat farm five kilometers from the Syrian border. Thermal imaging of the location has confirmed a concrete bunker under the farmhouse itself. That's where we assume his weapons cache is stored. It's a perfect cover."

The other men shook their heads. The lieutenant knew that, like him, they couldn't believe such a large cache of weapons had been under their noses this whole time.

"We'll HALO in south of the compound and hump it through the dried wadis until we reach the farm," continued Donovan. "Once there, we split into two two-man teams. We enter hot, clearing the main house one room at a time. After we secure the package—code named Viper—we'll exit the way we came in, leaving an IR beacon for the cleanup."

"Are we relying on bunker bombs to take out the cache, sir?" asked Miller.

Donovan nodded. "Yes, Master Chief," he confirmed. "These orders are straight from Admiral Garrow. It's a snatch and grab of the biggest fish, men. We're not there for his toys. That clear?"

"Hoorah!" the men all grunted in unison.

"This'll be Close Quarters Combat, men. Kit out what you'll need for CQB," said Donovan. He looked down at his wrist and checked the time on his grandfather's watch. "We're wheels up in three hours. Dismissed."

As the others began to file out of the tent, Agent Upton walked over to Donovan. "Not a bad plan, kid," Upton grunted and picked one of the maps off the table. "But a wadi becomes a choke point if things get hot."

Lieutenant Commander Donovan snatched the map away. He didn't have to listen to some CIA agent lecture him on combat. "Don't worry about us," said Donovan. He glared at Upton. "We'll extract through the palm grove if we need to."

The agent shrugged. "Fine," he said. "Sounds like you've got it covered. Just that—well, we've had reports recently of mines hidden in heavy vegetation like this."

"I said we've got it!" Donovan snapped.

"What's your beef, kid?" asked Upton.

"If I'd followed you back there with Hakedam," said Donovan, "there wouldn't be any plan."

"What do you mean?" asked Agent Upton. "Oh, I see. You think my being honest to Hakedam was a mistake? Is that it?"

"That wasn't honesty," said Donovan, raising his voice. "That was plain insulting. You almost cost us the intel. Sir."

"Kid," Upton began. He leaned over the desk and started rifling through the stack of paperwork and images. "I've been in this game a long time. The man took a shine to you the second your boots hit the dirt. I saw it as a weakness and exploited it. It was a classic good cop, bad cop scheme."

"You were playing him?" Donovan asked, a bit shocked.

"Donovan, the man is a murderer and a bully," said Agent Upton. "If I don't play his game—you know, stoop to his level of slime—we'd never get anything out of him."

"If you think he's so corrupt, why are we dealing with him?" asked Donovan.

"It's a pendulum here, kid," Upton replied. "Today, Hakedam's in a power position and has what we need.

Tomorrow it'll be someone else, and Hakedam will be on the hit list. Either way, we don't get to deal with just nice people in this business."

Upton's schemes didn't sit well with Donovan. He didn't like playing games. He was too aware of all the collateral damage Upton's clever tactics could cause to innocent civilians.

"The Iraqi people are counting on us," said Donovan. "How can we change a world that still relies on bullies and bad guys to make the country run? How is that fair to the people we're trying to protect and liberate?"

"It's not fair," said Agent Upton. "But we're enforcers of policy, not creators. Wanna change the world, kid? Become President. Until then, we all follow orders, so go follow yours."

Donovan stormed out of the tent.

Taking a second to breathe, Agent Upton stared at the intel he'd help deliver to the SEALs still projected on the screen. He grinned.

"No arguments there, kid," he said.

***

Several hours later, Lieutenant Commander Donovan and his men hit the drop zone near Tal Afar. Like an undiscovered oasis, the palm grove sat in the center of a valley surrounded by hills of sand. Dried riverbeds, or wadis, led into the oasis like natural roads. All the team needed to do was to follow them in.

The edge of the palm grove extended past the mountain range to the south, but was closer to the goat farm. Donovan thought it wise to avoid detection by parachuting in farther north and hoofing it.

The moon had set and the desert was pitch black. It was a perfect night to carry out a covert insertion. Noise and light discipline were in effect, so no one spoke. If they needed to speak to one another, they'd use hand signals. Their gear, from straps to ammo pouches, was taped down to prevent any unwanted noises.

Holding up a closed fist, Donovan halted the team. He took a pair of small binoculars from his bag. Night became day as the infrared unit magnified the light and showed him the goat farm in the distance. The so-called farmhouse was a smaller building than they had planned on. It was nestled right in the far northern end of the grove.

Two Iraqi men patrolled the building, AK-47s in their clutches.

Waving one hand in the air while making fists and walking signals with his fingers, Donovan told the SEALs what to do next. Quickly and quietly, the squad broke into their two-man fire-teams: Kaili with Williams and Miller with Donovan. They headed toward the farmhouse, their silenced M4 shorties in their hands.

After moving into place, each team crouched in the high cover of the elephant grass on the edge of the palm grove.

They waited for their chance to remove the sentries. The grass sighed softly in the night breeze.

One of the guards strode past Master Chief Miller. The sailor was camouflaged in the moonless night. Like a tiger, Miller pounced, wrapping his arms around the man's neck and immediately taking him to the ground. Miller had expertly incapacitated the guard with a choke hold.

As the other guard passed, Kaili rose from his hidden position. Like Miller had, he blood-choked the Iraqi to the ground, sending him into unconsciousness in seconds. Both men quickly zip-tied the soldiers' wrists and legs.

Gathering back up, Miller with Donovan, Williams with Kaili, they moved toward the house. Team 1 to the back entrance, Team 2 to the side door.

Huddled near the side entrance, Donovan placed a brick of plastic explosive with a remote trigger on the wooden door's lock. He stepped back. Cradled in his hand was the detonator. He counted down the seconds on his grandfather's watch.

At the rear of the house, Kaili and Williams did the same.

"Three...two...BREACH!" Donovan said.

Clicking the detonators almost simultaneously, the SEALs blew open the doors to the small farmhouse. They rushed inside, their M4s up and ready. Donovan entered first and went left. Miller came in behind and broke right.

They were in a living room. The furnishings were minimal and the trappings light. This was purely a flop house, where the men slept after their black-market runs between countries. Small mattresses covered with dirty sheets lay on the floor.

In front of them, two Iraqi men exploded through the doorway, their guns raised and firing. In a flash, Miller and Donovan opened fire, blasting the men off their feet with short, controlled bursts from their machine guns.

The SEALs moved deeper into the house. At the back, Kaili and Williams did the same, their weapons raised. They came through the kitchen, but no one was there.

The men moved cautiously to the next room.

Both teams quickly worked their way toward the middle of the house and entered the dining room.

Two waiting gunmen turned and opened fire on Donovan and Miller, causing them to shrink back through the doorway. Kaili and Williams came up quickly behind them. Rifles raised, muzzle flash illuminated the Iraqi men's faces as their bodies jerked and fell to the deck. Perfectly placed shots from Fire Team 1 dropped the terrorists in a heartbeat.

"Clear!" Williams yelled as Donovan and Miller entered.

At the table, his hands in the air, sat Kasieem. "I surrender!"

Kaili threw the man to the floor. He forced Kasieem's hands behind his back and secured them with a zip-tie. Williams scoped the rest of the house.

Master Chief Miller looked over at Donovan and shook his head. "Seem too easy to you?" Miller asked his commanding officer.

Donovan nodded and looked around the room. "Yeah, only six guys and Kasieem?" he said. "Maybe we're missing something."

"Sir!" Williams called.

Donovan turned and ran to his teammate.

In the center of the room, a trap door was open leading down into the darkness. Donovan and Williams looked at each other in confusion.

"Where's that lead to?" Donovan asked.

"I think it's the access hatch to the weapons cache, sir," Williams said, eyeing the trapdoor nervously.

"Then we'd better I.D. it," Donovan said. "After you." He waved a hand toward the hole.

"Thanks, sir," Williams said sarcastically. Carefully, he dropped inside the trapdoor.

"Well?" Donovan yelled down to him.

"Can't see a thing. Electrics are out," Williams called up from the blackened hole.

"Here," Donovan said, dropping his grandfather's lighter. "What do you see now, Williams?"

A flickering yellow glow shone from the hole in the floor. All Donovan could see were gray concrete steps leading down.

Finally, Williams yelled back. "Nothing, sir! It's just a big, empty bunker."

Confused and angry, Donovan ordered him to come back. They both reunited with the rest of the team.

"What the heck is going on, sir?"Williams asked.

Donovan shook his head. "I dunno, but we did our job and we're outta here," he said. Then the four men, package in tow, moved out of the farmhouse.

Outside, Donovan and the men regrouped. Kasieem was still their prisoner.

Miller turned on a small infrared LED light and towed it onto the roof of the farmhouse. "IR's set, sir," he said.

"Then we'll extract the way we came in," Donovan said as he pointed at the wadi. "Seahawk's gonna pick us up on the far end where we landed. We'll retrieve our gear and—"

Donovan's shoulder jerked, catching him off balance. He spun 180 degrees and crumpled to the deck!

"Sir!" Miller yelled, kneeling beside Donovan.

Dust clouds puffed up as bullets poured toward them from the wadi.

"Snipers!"Williams exclaimed.

"I'm—I'm okay, Master Chief," Donovan growled as he and the others took cover behind some trees and returned fire.

"Covering fire, Williams!" Miller ordered.

He and Kaili both crouched behind palm trees and fired back at the Iraqis.

The sound of whizzing bullets filled the air. Firecracker pops echoed around them. AK-47 bullets flew through the palm grove. The SEALs were pinned to the ground. They had to formulated a plan.

"Vest took the brunt of it," Donovan said. He coughed.

"Thank God! Last thing I wanna be doin' is carrying you around again." Miller smiled.

"Palm grove!" Donovan ordered. "We'll go north, have the helo pick us up on the other side."

"Right!" Miller said as he stood, weapon in hand.

One by one, the SEALs peeled off, providing cover for each other as they made their way deeper into the palm grove.

"I count thirty, maybe more, dug in on the south ridge," Kaili said as he loaded his weapon. "We're gonna need some help out here, sir!"

After pulling up a small radio from his daypack, Donovan keyed the handset. "Home Plate, this is Black Mamba," he said. "We have walked into an ambush, I need CAS at 1-8-5 degrees, seven hundred meters up the hillside from my position, over."

Bullets embedded themselves in the tree trunk Donovan was hiding behind. After a second, Upton's voice came on the line. "Hang tight, Black Mamba. Incoming," crackled the radio.

A gray shape flew out of the darkness. It swooped past the SEALs and toward the terrorists. In a flash, the UAV Predator drone shot twin Heckfire missiles from under its wings.

Hot red flashes of fire appeared on the mountainside. Suddenly, the shooting stopped.

"Kick butt and take names, Home Plate! And thanks!" Donovan radioed. The SEALs ran deeper into the overgrown cover of thick grass and towering palm trees.

One quick stride at a time, they fled the blazing scene. As they pushed farther into the oasis, Lester Donovan suddenly flashed back to his earlier conversation with Agent Upton.

Wait—what was it he said about the foliage? he thought. *Something about—*

Eyes going wide, Donovan turned to his men and shouted, "Freeze!"

It was too late. In that instant, Kaili's foot came down in just the right spot—a *click* rang out through the night. In a sudden, brilliant flash of yellow and orange, he was propelled five feet into the air.

He'd stepped on a land mine.

The bottom half of his leg was gone, vaporized by the mine's intense heat and fiery explosion. When he landed, he was completely unconscious.

"Kaili!" Williams yelled. He started running.

"No, don't!" Donovan ordered, but Williams ran to Kaili's side anyway. He knelt by Kaili and began first aid.

"No one move! We're in a mine field!" Donovan screamed. He glanced over at Kasieem and could swear the Iraqi was smiling. Donovan grabbed the radio. "Home Plate, Black Mamba, we are in the middle of a mine field and have no casualties. Request immediate extraction, over."

"Negative, Black Mamba," said the voice from the radio.

"What?!" shouted Donovan. "We're sitting ducks out here. We need immediate extraction."

"You need to clear the mine field before we can risk a rescue bird," said the radio operator. "Suggest to traverse to the north. MEDIVAC will meet you there, out."

Donovan shook his head. "Roger. Out."

"So?" Miller asked.

"They won't risk the helo," said Donovan. "We need to walk out of here on our own."

"Then let the Iraqi take point, sir," Miller suggested as he shoved Kasieem forward.

"No, we can't. If he dies, we have no leads," Donovan said. "Then, even if we were able to get out of this, it would all be for nothing."

"Better than one of us getting blown to heck," Miller said.

"No, Master Chief!" shouted the lieutenant commander. "It's not right and I won't do it! I'm not stooping to their level."

A tense moment passed between the SEALs as Donovan racked his brain for a way out of the situation. "How's Kaili?" he asked.

Williams finished applying the tourniquet and looked up at Donovan. "He's bad. We need to get him outta here, sir," Williams said.

"Okay," Donovan said, rising to his feet. "I'll take point."

"No way!" Miller protested, but Donovan waved him off.

"This is the only way," Donovan said. "I take point. You all step exactly where I step. We walk out of here and call for extraction on the other side of the grove."

Donovan took a deep breath. He turned north, looking down at the ground, wondering where to start. The first step, Donovan thought as he lifted his foot off the ground, is always the hardest. His boot was shaking. He could barely hold it up long enough to place it back down.

Finally, he stepped.

Donovan smiled. "Let's move out, Master Chief, and keep him close." He nodded over at Kasieem.

Kasieem was no longer smiling. Now, it seemed he was just as scared to die as the rest of them.

Miller laughed. "Don't worry, sir, I don't think he'll be a problem now."

Miller followed behind Donovan, stepping exactly where the officer's footfalls landed and dragging Kasieem along.

Williams hoisted his Hawaiian teammate over his shoulders in a fireman's carry. Kaili awoke, groggy and pumped full of morphine, and looked around lazily.

"Williams, be careful, man..." he said. "I think there're mines out here." Then he passed out again.

***

After what felt like a lifetime, the SEALs, moving slowly through the underbrush, came to the edge of the palm grove. A sea of sand spread out before them.

"Home Plate, Black Mamba," Donovan radioed. "We are out of the minefield and en route to the extraction point. Request immediate evac, over."

The radio hissed. "Roger, Black Mamba," Upton's voice said, "you should be able to see them now."

Upton was right. The Seahawk was a small dot on the horizon, but it was on its way. Upton had sent the vehicle out early in anticipation of the SEALs getting to the MEDIVAC point quickly.

All in all, the CIA agent may be a brash, arrogant Spook, Donovan thought, *but he's a good man.*

When the helicopter landed, the SEALs rushed forward. A corpsman jumped out, grabbed hold of Kaili, and took charge of him. One after another, the SEALs boarded, and in an instant the helo powered up and dusted off. The massive rotor blade kicked up storms of sand as it lifted into the air. Its nose dipped, turned toward the west, and disappeared into the sun.

***

The sun was beginning to rise over FOB as Donovan sat alone outside, watching the golden rays of morning break over the horizon. Though the mission had technically been a success, he felt like a failure. Kaili would live, but he'd lost the lower half of his leg and his career in the Navy SEALs was over.

After hitting the tarmac, the team had gone through debriefing via satellite linkup with the admirals at SOCOM. Donovan was found non-culpable of any wrongdoing for the incident. But it was his command decision that had gotten a good man and friend injured and almost killed. He couldn't let go of that.

"Feeling sorry for yourself?" a voice called from behind.

Donovan turned to see Upton standing there, holding out a bottle of water for him.

"I know, I'm a jerk," said the agent.

"And then some," Donovan snapped. "What do you want?"

"To tell you we debriefed Kasieem. Looks like someone robbed his stash two days before we got there and killed most of his men, which is why no one was really there when you got there." Upton sat next to Donovan and looked out at the rising sun.

"He say who did it?" Donovan asked.

Upton nodded and smiled.

Donovan figured it out immediately. "Hakedam?"

"Yep, the police chief. We figure he was trying to cut out his competition, which is why he called us in. He gets the guns, we get Kasieem and destroy his operation, and Hakedam becomes the only black marketer in town makin' out like a bandit." Upton laughed.

"Not a bad plan." Donovan chuckled.

"By the way, you did a good job out there," Upton said.

Donovan shot Upton a nasty look. "That is a really crappy thing to joke about," he said.

"No, seriously," Upton said. "Sounds like it got really major out there. Master Chief told me what you did, leading your team out of that mine field."

"We had to get out of there," Donovan replied.

"Took real bravery to not lose it and break down," Upton said. "You showed some great leadership, and whether or not we got played by Hakedam, your guys did the job perfectly."

"It shouldn't have gone that way," Donovan said, glancing over at Upton. "I missed something you were trying to tell me because I let my anger and ego get in the way. And because of that, a good man was almost killed."

"You're right," Upton said.

"Don't sugarcoat things much, do you?" Donovan said.

"Nope," Upton said. "Things can go wrong even if you do everything right. We got the bad guy, and we didn't lose anyone. Sometimes that's all you can ask for."

"It's still not right," Donovan said. "If I had only listened, that kid would still be walking."

Upton stood and nudged Donovan with the water bottle. Donovan took it. "At least he's still breathing," Upton said. "And next time, you'll know better."

Upton walked off, leaving Donovan alone with his thoughts.

Donovan stood and stared at the water bottle in his hand. Water. It was a precious thing out here, in a country in the middle of the sand. Precious, like a pair of legs to stand on. Like being able to hold up your head for a mission well done. Like leading your men to safety even though your heart is pounding in your chest, and you're as frightened as a little kid.

He drank. As the first light of a new day crossed his face, Donovan pondered his future and the future of his family.

M. ZACHARY SHERMAN

Sherman is a veteran of the United States Marine Corps. He has written comics for Marvel, Radical, Image, and Dark Horse. His recent work includes *America's Army: The Graphic Novel*, *Earp: Saint for Sinners*, and the second book in the *SOCOM: SEAL Team Seven* trilogy.

AUTHOR Q&A

Q: Any relation to the Civil War Union General William Tecumseh Sherman?

A: Yes, indeed! I was one of the only members of my family lineage to not have some kind of active duty military participation—until I joined the U.S. Marines at age 28.

Q: Why did you decide to join the U.S. Marine Corps? How did the experience change you?

A: I had been working at the same job for a while when I thought I needed to start giving back. The biggest change for me was the ability to see something greater than myself; I got a real sense of the world going on outside of just my immediate, selfish surroundings. The Marines helped me to grow up a lot. They taught me the focus and discipline that helped get me where I am today.

Q: When did you decide to become a writer?

A: I've been writing all my life, but the first professional gig I ever had was a screenplay for Illya Salkind (*Superman 1–3*) back in 1995. But it was a secondary profession, with small assignments here and there, and it wasn't until around 2005 that I began to get serious.

Q: Has your military experience affected your writing?

A: Absolutely, especially the discipline I have obtained. Time management is key when working on projects, so you must be able to govern yourself. In regards to story, I've met and been with many different people, which enabled me to become a better storyteller through character.

Q: Describe your approach to the Bloodlines series. Did personal experiences in the military influence the stories?

A: Yes and no. I didn't have these types of experiences in the military, but the characters are based on real people I've encountered. And those scenarios are all real, just the characters we follow have been inserted into the time lines. I wanted the stories to fit into real history, real battles, but have characters we may not have heard of be the focus of those stories. I've tried to retell the truth of the battle with a small change in the players.

Q: Any future plans for the Bloodlines series?

A: There are so many battles through history that people don't know about. If they hadn't happened, the world would be a much different place! It's important to hear about these events. If we can learn from history, we can sidestep the mistakes we've made as we move forward.

Q: What's your favorite book? Favorite movie? Favorite video game?

A: My favorite book is *The Maltese Falcon* by Dashiell Hammett. I love a good mystery with hard-boiled detectives! As for movies, hands-down it's *Raiders of the Lost Ark*. It is a fantastic story of humanity winning out over evil and the characters are real people thrown into impossible odds. Lots of fun! As for games, there are way too many to mention, but I love sci-fi shooters and first-person games.

U.S. MILITARY CONFLICTS

WORLD WAR II

In 1939, Adolf Hitler and his German army invaded the country of Poland. This ruthless dictator viewed Germans as the "master race". He hoped to exterminate all Jews from Europe and eventually rule the world. Some countries, including Italy and Japan, joined his evil efforts. They were known as the Axis powers. Others chose to fight against him and his Nazi regime. Those countries, which included Great Britain, France, Russia, and the United States, were known as the Allies. To stop German expansion and the genocide of European Jews, the Allied troops could not fail.

KOREAN WAR

For thousands of years, people have fought over Korea. From 1910 until the end of World War II, Japan controlled the entire peninsula. However, after the war, Korea was divided into two parts. Russia controlled the northern half of the peninsula, and the United States controlled the southern half. Three years later, the two halves became independent nations — North Korea and South Korea. But their troubles were just beginning. On June 25, 1950, North Korea, led by their communist ruler Kim Il Sung, attacked the South. This action started what would become the Korean War.

WORLD WAR II
(1939-1945)

KOREAN WAR
(1950-1953)

VIETNAM WAR
(1955-1975)

VIETNAM WAR

The Vietnam War began as a conflict over what kind of government the country would have: communist or capitalist. At the start of the war in 1959, South Vietnam and North Vietnam were two separate countries. South Vietnam battled the communist Vietcong of the South and the communists of North Vietnam. The Vietcong and North Vietnam wanted to unite the two countries into one communist nation. They were backed by the Soviet Union and China. Under the leadership of President Lyndon Johnson, the United States supported South Vietnam with money and troops.

AFGHAN WAR

On September 11, 2001, the terrorist group Al-Qaeda attacked the United States, hijacking four commercial airliners and flying three of them into buildings along the East Coast. President George W. Bush and the U.S. military responded quickly. On October 7, 2001, they began Operation Enduring Freedom, attempting to shut down Al-Qaeda hideouts in Afghanistan and capture their leader, Osama Bin Laden. In recent years, the military campaign has evolved into a counter-insurgency operation — tactics to keep the Afghan government and citizens in favor of U.S. policy.

IRAQ WAR

In 2002, the U.N. Security Council passed Resolution 1441, forcing Iraq to comply with the U.N. in a search for weapons of mass destruction (WMDs) in Iraqi facilities. The Iraqi government complied, allowing the U.N. Monitoring, Verification, and Inspection Commission (UNMOVIC) complete access to their country. However, the UNMOVIC was unable to locate any evidence of WMDs, and a U.S.-run Iraqi survey group determined that all of Iraq's nuclear, chemical, and biological programs had ended by 1991. Despite these findings, the invasion was undertaken on March 20th, 2003, by order of the U.S. President, George W. Bush and the U.K. Prime Minister, Tony Blair.

AFGHAN WAR
(2001-Present)

IRAQ WAR
(2003-2011)

BLOODLINES
HEART OF WAR